Book One in the Twelve Cursed Maidens series

MAIDEN TOMB

Would you marry the first stranger who came along to free your sisters from imprisonment?

CYNTHIA SALLY HAGGARD

ISBN: 979-8985496963
Enquiries: greetings@cynthiasallyhaggard.com
Published by Cynthia Sally Haggard, Washington DC, USA
www.cynthiasallyhaggard.com
Edited by Gabriella Guiet, Allison Heddon, Leah Parkhouse and Rachel Froelich
Cover Design by Katie Birks of Katie Birks Branding & Design

PRAISE FOR MAIDEN TOMB

What readers have to say ~

"*Maiden Tomb* is a shadowy, spellbinding tale where sisterhood and secrets collide in a world that makes freedom feel like a distant dream."—Leah P.

"*Maiden Tomb* is not a retelling per se. Instead it combines elements of Greek Mythology with the tale of *The Twelve Dancing Princesses* into a unique collage that will appeal to readers who enjoy Madeline Miller's *Circe*, and Naomi Novak's *Spinning Silver*."—Catherine H.

"*Maiden Tomb* features a wide cast of characters, each playing an intricate role. Worry not about keeping the twelve sisters separate, for Haggard has sharply characterized each, from the brittle eldest sister to the sunny youngest."—Katharine M.

"For fans of Fantasy and Greek Mythology, *Maiden Tomb* delivers a captivating tale of sisterly love, mad kings and undercover suitors."—Marley V.

"In a world steeped in myth and mystery, twelve princesses are locked in a tower. Their peaceful captivity is shattered when the sisters begin dying under mysterious circumstances." —Stephanie R.

"*Maiden Tomb* is the first installment of *The Twelve Cursed Maidens* series. Readers in high school and above will be captivated by the writing style and quick pace." —Tiffany E.

AWARDS FOR CYNTHIA SALLY HAGGARD

Thwarted Queen
IPPY Gold Medal for Audiobook Fiction
May 2021

Farewell My Life
Independent Press Award for Women's Fiction
April 2021
New York City Big Book Award Distinguished Favorite
November 2019

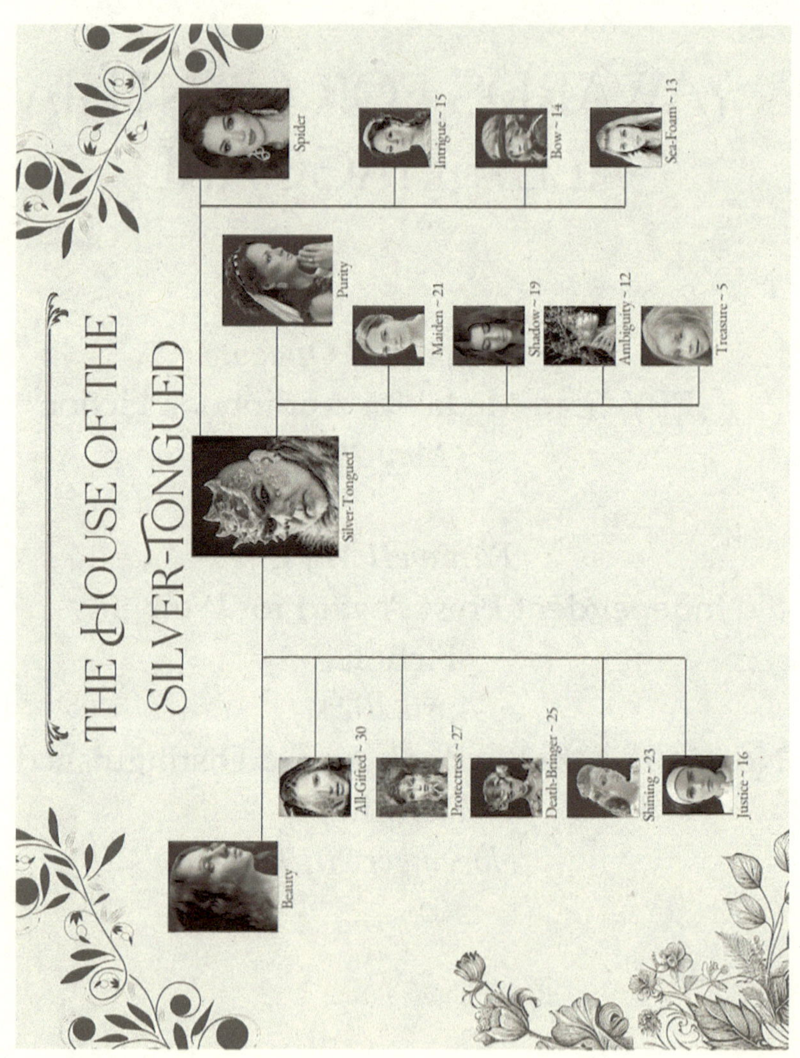

THE HOUSE OF THE
SILVER-TONGUED
Beauty
Silver-Tongued
Spider
All-Gifted ~ 30
Protectress ~ 27
Death-Bringer ~ 25
Shining ~ 23
Justice ~ 16
Purity
Maiden ~ 21
Shadow ~ 19
Ambiguity ~ 12
Treasure ~ 5
Intrigue ~ 15
Bow ~ 14
Sea-Foam ~ 13

Lady All-Gifted's Journey from Sikelia to Constantinople

Prologue~

The Twelve Mysterious Daughters

Playful speaks

In the past week or so since we've arrived, life has taken on a predictable rhythm. I spend the mornings entertaining the ladies of the castle, with the lyre, my singing, playing knucklebones, and listening to their gossip. Truth to tell, nothing they say is particularly interesting as high-born ladies spend their time inside. When they are not diverting themselves with such pastimes as I provide, they are spinning, weaving, running the household, and caring for their children. They talk incessantly about their children. They know little of the outside world.

I escape after the midday meal, taking advantage of the ladies' habit of resting as the sun's chariot crests at the highest point of the day. While they sleep, I head out into the scorching countryside looking for Father.

We sit together in the shade, while Father does some task, usually repairing something, while I tell him everything I've learned the evening before. It is not that hard. Because I am small, and people are now familiar with my face, no one pays me any mind as I take my seat at the bench that runs along the side of the huge table where all the working folk of the castle eat their meals.

Father has told me never to be inquisitive, but I am dying to know more about the twelve mysterious ladies locked up in the castle tower, the ones people whisper about behind their hands when they think no-one is noticing.

As the light of the sun drains from the sky, the king's men sink lower onto wooden benches eating dish after dish: quail, pheasant, peacock, duck, eggs, bread, olive oil, wine, and olives. The noise of seven hundred men sharing jokes, laughing, and swilling wine reverberates around the hall.

Finally, I can take it no more. "Is it true what they say about the King's daughters?"

The grizzled stranger on the bench next to me wipes the grease off his mouth with the back of a hand and spits out an olive pit.

"Where've you popped up from? You shouldn't be here. You're only a young lad."

I am used to these remarks, After I left home I took a ship that was blown off course, taking me west to the land of the Italoi. I had to beg for money in the streets and in the taverns, and it was not long before I heard news of Father, who was sailing to the west of this land.

And so I made my way across a range of steep mountains before coming down to a lush plain. Playing my lyre to entertain strangers, I followed their directions to the sea, to a wide bay within sight of a simmering, high, conical-shaped mountain.

And there, in a tavern, I met Father.

Now we are traveling home together. But Father is not here on the bench beside me, as he should be, but outside at a nearby farm pretending to be a stable hand.

This is one of Father's clever strategies. He is a master at extracting information. He calls his strategy "divide and conquer" and it means that I must use my lyre to find a berth for the night in some local chieftain's house. This is not usually difficult, especially if there are ladies around because for some reason, they always want to pet me.

Meanwhile, Father finds work on the outside as a shepherd, farmhand, or stable boy. By concealing his origins and pretending to be dumb, drunk, or both, Father is able to overhear a great many things. We have a plan to meet every day at noon, I escaping the blandishments of the ladies to visit the local farm for milk, cheese, eggs, where I could happen upon the new stable boy, farmhand, or shepherd.

The only fly in the ointment is my age. I am only twelve years old and to my great annoyance, I look it. So, Father made me memorize some phrases to offer when this issue arises.

"Father is here with me but is suffering with an ache to his belly."

One sentence is usually enough for most people. Father has instructed me never to offer explanations that are not asked for as it only makes people more curious.

But this fellow is staring at me, waiting for more.

I turn my eyes down. "Father told me to eat supper and then berth with him in the stable yard."

"He's the new stable hand, is he?"

I nod.

"Much good he'll be with a bellyache."

I look up. "Do you have a remedy for that good sir?"

Father always stresses the importance of asking for advice when a conversation turns sour, as it flatters the vanity.

The fellow hawks and spits, rising from his seat. "You'll have to go to the kitchens for that, son." He ambles off.

I return to my meal, hoping the others will forget about me and the conversation I've just had. Fortunately, it is that time of the meal when men turn tipsy. Pretty soon they are laughing, singing, and telling dirty jokes. One song goes like this:

"There once was a king with twelve daughters—"

—"Twelve bee-yoo-tiful daughters" sing the others in an out-of-tune chorus.

"But he refused to marry them off—"

—"Twelve bee-yoo-tiful daughters"

"And why did he refuse to marry them off?"

—"Twelve bee-yoo-tiful daughters

"Because they would make unsuitable wives—"

—"Twelve bee-yoo-tiful daughters"

"The eldest is mad
The second is bad
The third is sad
The fourth too bold
The fifth too shrill
The sixth too shy
The seventh too just
While the eighth loves her father—too much Ha! Ha!
The eighth loves her father too much!
The ninth is a boy
The tenth a mermaid

The eleventh a goddess
While the twelfth has only five years, five years
The twelfth daughter has only five years."

"Do not touch!" yells someone to guffawing laughter.

The men pick up their song again:

"But the one you need to watch for is number four, number four,
The one you need to watch for is number four.
For the fourth daughter is a very naughty girl
With large bold eyes and a nearly naked form—"

This goes on for some time. The fourth daughter seems to fascinate the men. I chew thoughtfully. Somehow, I must find a way of meeting her.

I turn to another man. "Is it true he locked all twelve of his daughters up in a high tower?"

The man nods.

"Why are they going on about the fourth daughter? I thought it was the eldest who dishonored the family name—"

"Keep your voice down," hisses the fellow. He looks around and then stares back at me from under bushy brows. "Your information is quite good, boy. Most of what you say is true."

"Which part is false?"

The fellow rises to his feet. "If you'll take my advice, you'll keep your mouth shut. Folk pay with their lives by asking too many questions." He glances around and draws his forefinger across his throat.

"But—" I gesture to the men singing lustily.

"They're drunk."

"But—" I say again. But the man vanishes into the press of sweaty male bodies.

Outside, it is a lovely evening with cool puffs of air wafting across my cheeks. The castle tower stands up like a finger, a beckoning, a warning, that people can see for miles around. If their eyesight is good, they will see a window set high in the tower, just underneath the tiled roof. On a fine day, the window unlatched, the wind carries the sound of voices, the high sound of girls' voices gossiping, chattering, giggling. Now, on this late summer evening, someone closes that high window shut. I catch a glimpse of a heart-shaped face with deep-set dark-grey eyes, and light-brown hair drawn back into a braid. Which daughter could she be? Not number four, for she is dressed modestly in a light woolen robe dyed a soft grey to match her eyes.

I lift my head to the moon, a thin fingernail of a crescent. A shiver runs up my spine. Something is going to happen within the month, I can feel it. This place hums with suppressed tensions.

Father will be so interested when I see him tomorrow.

ONE~

SEA CREATURES

The Tower of the Castle
Sikelia
Late Summer 840 CE

Justice speaks

I am unknown, but not unknowable. I have my hopes, but I am silent. I sit and bide my time, one among twelve, spinning an even thread, or weaving, or embroidering Intrigue's robes, watching and listening as life ebbs around me, like waves crashing on a dull grey shore. No one notices the shore that they stand on, they are mesmerized by those waves. But the shore provides the stability, the foundation.

I am the forgettable sister. The constant, grey presence that melts into the grey wall behind me. With sisters like All-Gifted, Protectress, and Death-Bringer, who could remember me?

My sisters are like sea creatures, each one a different color.

All-Gifted, the eldest, is as brown as mud. Everyone thinks her mad because she mutters over that brown cauldron of hers.

Protectress is the color of dried blood.

Death-Bringer, the light green of bleached winter leaves.

Shining, of course, is as shining as her name, a magnet for the male gaze.

Maiden, the tart green of an unripe apple.

Intrigue, the fierce orange of fire, Father's seeming favorite.

Shadow is unseen.

And I, Justice, am grey.

The others are too young to count.

We sit here, locked in the top of a high tower, awaiting Father's pleasure. It has been ten long years. Father rules the country of Sikelia as King Silver-Tongued, the first of that name. Many wonder why he has locked us up. But no one seems to know.

Our stolen years are something no one speaks about. But it is a constant burden for the elder daughters.

All-Gifted has now thirty years,
Protectress is twenty-seven,
Death-Bringer, twenty-five,
Shining, twenty-three,
Maiden, twenty-one,
Shadow, nineteen,
and I, Justice am sixteen.

Even Intrigue is beginning to feel her years at the tender age of fifteen, for it is the custom in our land for girls to marry at first blood. By that measure, eleven of Father's twelve daughters should be wed. Instead, we live in a cloud, in a conspiracy of silence, our lives not yet begun.

"She's going to eat me." Five-year-old Treasure's amber eyes look huge in her tiny face.

I kneel before her and take her hands in my own. "What do you mean dearest?"

Treasure points to All-Gifted's squat cauldron, seething softly in its corner. Every so often the lid lifts, sending out a coil of steam, greenish in color, sweetly sticky in its odor. It reminds me of pickled cucumbers.

"She's going to put me in that pot and boil me for supper."

"What makes you think that?"

Tears fill Treasure's eyes.

I hug her tight. "All-Gifted!" I call. There is no reply.

Tears stream down Treasure's face, blotting her creamy complexion with its tints of gold.

"Don't let her get me. I'll be good, I promise."

"Would you like to share my bed tonight?"

Treasure nods, sobs shaking her tiny frame. I draw a silken handkerchief from my sleeve and gently wipe away her tears. Then I take her by the hand, sit her on my bed, and undress her behind the bed curtains.

As I tell her a story, my sisters appear, one by one, for it is now the hour when the evening meal is served.

"What happened?" asks twelve-year-old Ambiguity.

"I don't know," I say. "I found her standing by All-Gifted's cauldron, saying she would be eaten for supper."

Twenty-three-year-old Shining-Light stifles a giggle. "All-Gifted is scary to look at," she remarks. "But she means so harm. She's just mad. Everyone knows that."

Nineteen-year-old Shadow rises from her bed, which is beside mine. "Why don't you go downstairs to eat?" she says in her thread-like whisper. "I'll take care of Treasure until you return."

I smile as I kiss my sister on the cheek. Shadow is so shy, she would be happy if she never had to eat downstairs. "I'll bring you something!" I call as I follow my ten sisters down those twisting, winding stairs.

TWO~

FATHER

Playful speaks

It is dusty and hot by the time I find Father. He beckons me inside the stable, the coolest place in this scorching heat. While we share a simple meal of bread, cheese, olives, and weak wine, I tell Father about the events of the previous night.

He frowns when I mention the question I asked last night about the twelve ladies.

"How many times have I asked you not to ask such questions? You'll only draw attention to yourself."

"But he was drunk," I lie.

"Hmm. Let's hope so," he replies, gnawing on his crust of bread.

No one looking at Father now would believe he is the King of Ithaca. With his washed-out clothes, his rough feet, his deep tan setting off the scars and lines that seam his face, he looks like a typical peasant. Even his slouch is convincing.

I look around. "Why are you doing this?" I whisper. "Why don't you come inside and meet the king in person?"

"Because he's mad," Father replies under his breath. "And mad people are unpredictable. I want to find out more about those daughters before I make my move."

"So, you are pleased?" I ask, happy that I've done something right.

Father gives me a look. "No, I am not. You should leave those delicate matters in my hands, son. Being inquisitive can only get you into trouble. And if you should find yourself in those madman's hands, life could become very dangerous."

I stare at him. "But what could he do? I am only a child."

Father thins his lips and turns away. "Just make sure you don't let that happen," he says gruffly.

There is a pause while I digest this latest nugget of information. Then I turn. "Did I tell you that I actually saw one of the daughters?"

Father frowns again. "Did she see you?"

"No. She was shutting the window up high in the tower. She was too far away to see me."

"What was she like?"

"She was dressed modestly in a fine woolen gown, with sinuous leaves surrounding the neckline. She had light-brown hair drawn back into a braid. But she was so lovely, her face—" I pause trying to find my words.

"Her face?" Prompts Father.

"It was shaped like an upside-down pear, with a pointed chin. And her eyes were large —"

"What color were her eyes?"

"Grey, not unlike the color of your eyes, Father."

"And you are sure she didn't see you?"

"No, Father. I was too far away."

"But you saw her very well indeed."

"Oh." My face warms.

"If you could see her so well as to give me such a detailed description, how do you know she couldn't see you just as well?"

I look at the ground, my face heating like bread in the oven. "I hadn't thought of that," I admit.

Father touches my arm. "You must be much more careful, son. You must assume that people are watching you all the time."

"But why would they do that?"

"Because you are a stranger."

"But no one notices me. I'm not important."

"No one *appears* to notice you," Father corrects. "But they are looking at you all the same. Make sure that you give them no reason to remember you." He puts his finger under my chin and tilts it up. I am forced to gaze into a pair of steely grey eyes. "Do I make myself clear?"

"Yes, Father," I murmur.

THREE~

All-Gifted's Bed

Justice speaks

Imagine twelve females locked together in a large, round room each night. From above, it looks like a pie cut into twelve slices. When Father made his decision to lock us up, All-Gifted and I were returning from Constantinople. In the scramble for beds, we come last.

Naturally, Intrigue has the bed nearest the door. Even at five, she knew how to bat her eyes at everyone to bend them to her will. All-Gifted's bed was placed opposite hers, the elder daughters following her in a counter-clockwise fashion: Protectress, followed by Death-Bringer, then Shining, then Maiden.

The bed on the other side of All-Gifted's was left empty. For me. For even then, they avoided All-Gifted. Shadow took the bed on the other side of mine, while the littlest ones clustered around Intrigue, their glamorous heroine.

Each pie-slice contains a canopied bed, a chest at the end of the bed for clothes, and a table with a mirror. All-Gifted's bed is clothed in heavy brown hemp, practical and long-lasting. Protectress's curtains are the blood-red silk of ambition. Death-Bringer has the washed-out green of grief. Shining's are the gold of desire. Maiden's are the green of hopeful spring whilst Shadow's are as black as night. I, Justice, have the silver-grey of a sword, whilst Intrigue has magnificent silver silk curtains embroidered all over with the moon and stars, and the glowing sun done in golden thread.

Protectress, Shining, Maiden, Intrigue, Sea-Foam and I strew our tables with herbs, hair-pins, hair-combs, jewels, perfume, ointments and flowers. But All-Gifted replaces her table with her cauldron. Death-Bringer has only a curl of black hair done up in a green ribbon on her table. Shadow's has a mask only, her favorite black cloak, which makes her looks almost invisible, secured in her chest. I have a sword, which I keep under my bed. Bow keeps her bow, arrows, arm-guards, wrist guards, goose feathers, and other archery tackle under her bed also. She is the only sister who doesn't actually spend much time in the tower. Dressed as a boy, she scrambles down a nearby tree and vanishes into the countryside, only returning in the evening. Ambiguity's table lies under a silver bowl filled with water, while Treasure has a collection of hand-me-down dolls.

On this particular afternoon, a day of muted light and rain, during that time of year when the trees begin to turn and the days shorten and cool, All-Gifted has been muttering more than usual.

I sit in my usual place on a window seat, high above the floor, embroidering. To get there, I have to part my curtains, tying them back with a strip of silver silk, put a stool on my bed, and edge up into the window seat. Once there, I can open or close the window as I choose, and I have light enough to work.

As the grey afternoon dims into the darker grey of night, I finish off a curving scallop on the bodice of Intrigue's latest gown. When I can no longer see, I fold the embroidery away and press my hands to my aching temples. But instead of climbing back down onto my bed to hurry downstairs for the evening meal, I sink lower into the stone window embrasure, becoming one with the shadows. What is All-Gifted doing?

She paces around her bed, arms held high, her voice lifted to an unearthly height. Higher and higher her voice keens. I shiver as silvery light slides along her arms. With a groan, the floor around her bed fissures, the bed tilts, hangs in the air, and then disappears into a puff of dust.

I stare in amazement. Why is this happening now? Here we have been, for ten long years, trapped in this round chamber. And now All-Gifted has found a way to escape? Is it because Purity the nun, Father's second wife, suddenly left, eased out, the gossips say, by scheming Intrigue? Is it because the seasons are turning, with Autumn in the air? Autumn is my favorite time, a season of fruitfulness, followed by the death of the Goddess. All-Gifted bears the sigil of Scorpio.

Where her bed has been, a set of stone stairs descends into blackness. All-Gifted sinks to the floor and moans, rocking back and forth. She seems inconsolable. And yet, she has been studying to be a priestess for years, poring over grimoires, mixing up brews in her cauldron, learning that peculiar kind of high singing that priestesses must study. She never, as far as I know, has been successful.

All-Gifted is a cruel name for my eldest sister for she is not gifted, and her many mistakes cause everyone to laugh, or treat her with scorn. The truth is, All-Gifted needs Morgana, the cunning woman whom Father employed to teach her herbal lore, charms, spells, shape-shifting, the use of the glamor, and sorcery. But Morgana is no longer with us. She left before Father locked us up. Before

All-Gifted became mad. And now what has she done?

I edge off my stone seat using the stool to drop softly onto my bed and climb down towards her. Sinking onto the floor I reach out my hand and put it on her shoulder. She doesn't move.

I don't know how long we crouch there on that stone floor, she and I, but at length, a pitter-pat of slippered feet followed by an iron shudder, as the heavy oak door is pushed inwards, heralding the arrival of our sisters. They trip in, giggling as usual, when all of a sudden they stop short.

As usual, Intrigue makes her way to the front.

"What have you done?" she demands.

Protectress and Death-Bringer follow next, Protectress yawning while Death-Bringer stares. Protectress's straight dark brows draw together in a frown as she points her finger at me as if I am a servant girl.

"You."

I fold my arms, glaring at her as I rise to my full height. (I am one of the tallest.)

"My name is Justice. Surely you can remember that."

Protectress ignores me, passing me by with a casual brush as if I were a tapestry or a piece of furniture. She collapses gracefully onto her bed, fanning herself languidly with a reed fan. The thick dark plaits that surround her head rise gently in the breeze, forked tongues flickering. She is beautiful, with her large blue eyes, regular features, strong jaw and that cleft above her chin. But it is a cold beauty. There is rarely any warmth emanating from her face. She would make a good statue.

"Did you cause those steps to appear?"

I remain silent, matching her glare for glare.

Death-Bringer continues to stare, her eyes radiating energy as they have not for many a long year. She is the tallest of us sisters, favoring the light green of spring leaves, the palest, palest green that makes her seem wraith-like and insubstantial. She points at the steps. "They lead down to my kingdom. Beware, my sisters—" Her whispery voice trails off.

"I don't know why I bother with Justice, she's too stupid to answer my questions," remarks Protectress, oblivious to the warning. She puts her fan down and rises. "All-Gifted? Is this your work?"

There is silence. Then slowly, All-Gifted rises to her feet. She straightens her usually humped back and draws her hands into the air. Her muddy brown garments vanish and in their place are folds of silvery-blue silk. Her greying hair lightens into an ash blond. A silver diadem holds her hair back. Her eyes shine dark blue as she smiles at us.

I can't stop staring. As a young beauty, All-Gifted had been blessed with red-gold hair, blue-green eyes, and white skin. Now, she looks completely different. She must be getting good at using the glamor. It can be used for extreme kinds of transformation, for shape-shifting into different animals, plants, or people, or for more subtle changes. Why my sister has chosen to turn herself into her rival, Empress Theodora, famed for her dark blue eyes and ash-blond hair, is beyond my comprehension. Had she intended to do that? But All-Gifted is lifting her arms.

"Sisters! Hear me! After many long years, I have finally succeeded in setting us free. Follow me, and I will lead you out of this dungeon. I will set you free from Father's snares. All of you, yes every one of you will be able to lead the life the goddess meant you to have."

Everyone gazes at her. All-Gifted has finally come into her own. She is beautiful, she is powerful, she is a princess, the eldest lady of the land.

Finally, she is ready to take her place as sovereign lady, brushing aside all those who would try to take it from her.

I turn to look at my fifteen-year-old half-sister, Father's favorite. But Intrigue is too astonished to reply.

"Come!" says All-Gifted beckoning. And following her, we fly down the stairs, Death-Bringer trailing us in the rear.

FOUR~

CERES ROCK

Justice continues her story

I huddle together with the others staring up at the moon that blazes across the sky. My sisters flew out of the tower so precipitously they've not thought to put on their cloaks, but stand there in their silken robes shivering. The moon gleams largely on that outcropping of Ceres rock, named for our mother Demeter.

Turning slowly, I see our castle thrust out behind us, its turret issuing a challenge across the peaceful countryside.

"Where are we?" Intrigue's high voice breaks the silence.

All-Gifted climbs to the top of the rock and faces us.

"Ceres rock, the door to the Underworld," she proclaims, her voice echoing into the quietness.

"Are we going to die?" squeaks one of my younger half-sisters. It is hard to tell which one as they cluster like doves around their heroine Intrigue.

"It's too cold out here," says Protectress, her deep voice rumbling like thunder. "I'm going back for my cloak."

"What are we going to do when Father finds out?" Maiden turns to follow.

All-Gifted points a finger at them. They freeze in mid-pose, unable to speak.

"We are all in this together, my sisters."

I peer at them. When she raises the spell, they are going to be furious.

"No one leaves this place until I say so," says All-Gifted.

"But what are you going to *do*?" Intrigue steps forward.

"I am going to set you free." All-Gifted raises her hands. "Look at me. I am a woman of middling years, yet I have no husband or children. Do you want to be like me? Do you want to spend the best years of your life moldering away in a tower, waiting for the prince that never comes?"

I stare at her, mesmerized. I have no idea why Father locked us up. It happened ten years ago, when All-Gifted and I returned from the Bride Show in Constantinople. And yet, I know it is unusual for a father to treat his daughters such. I am told it is the custom for a man of stature, such as our father King Silver-Tongued, to seek suitable young men for his daughters to marry: for gentlemen of wealth, power, land, and a distinguished lineage, so that the match may bring honor to the young woman's family. Yet Father never speaks of such matters, not to his advisors, not to my sisters, not to me. This is the first time anyone has spoken of it.

Why Father is so reluctant to marry us off, I am not too sure. I have heard many rumors over the years, gossip about All-Gifted's strange ways, Protectress's ruthless cruelty, Death-Bringer's unwavering melancholy, Shining's wild nature. Accordingly, no sensible man would want my sisters as wives.

At that point, my informant favors me with a meaningful look.

"But you, Lady Justice, are different. You are a lady, just like your dear mother. May fortune favor you with a husband!"

"Father has a brilliant marriage planned for *me*." Intrigue's penetrating voice jolts me from my thoughts.

Well, of course he would. Intrigue is his favorite daughter, the only one he deigns to speak with, while his eleven other daughters are left to guess his intentions. She steps next to All-Gifted, her silken robes lifting in the light breeze, the embroidery I'd taken such pains over gleaming in the silvery light. All-Gifted towers over her, but if Intrigue is intimidated, she doesn't show it. She turns to the younger ones.

"Don't listen to her, she's jealous. Just because she was rejected at the Bride Show doesn't mean to say we have to follow her. I suggest we go back and get into our beds. It's cold, and Father would be displeased if he knew we were out here."

All-Gifted barks a harsh laugh.

"So," she says. "Father has marriage plans for *you,* Intrigue." She folds her arms. "Now why would you believe that?"

"He told me so."

"Who is this suitor?" I move towards Intrigue.

Intrigue bends her head, a flush mounting her cheek.

"What is his name?" I ask, my voice resonating off the rock. "Come Intrigue, we are all most anxious to hear."

"I don't know."

"You don't know? How can that be?"

Intrigue remains silent, clenching her slender fingers into a fist.

"Did Father actually say he was going to marry you off?"

Intrigue lifts her chin and stares at me. "He did."

"Did he make a promise to you?"

Into the silence that follows, a sharp gust skirls the leaves of the olive trees silver-green, silver-green, silver-green.

"He never actually promised anything, did he?" remarks All-Gifted. She laughs harshly. "It seems Father treats his daughters alike. I am twice your age, and many a time I thought a suitor had come to set me free. But nothing ever came to pass."

Intrigue studies her slippers. Into the echoing silence that follows one thought nags at me: *Do I truly want a husband?* For the stories I've heard over the years, indicate that my long-dead Lady Mother was not happy in her marriage to Father. Indeed, I do not think any of his women were happy. Mother - Lady Beauty - gave Father five daughters: All-Gifted, Protectress, Death-Bringer, Shining, and me. She died of a fever shortly after I was born. Before her death, Father caused a scandal by abducting Purity the nun from the local convent. Purity was forced to give him four daughters: Maiden, Shadow, Ambiguity, and our youngest Treasure before she left. Along the way he took up with a dancer from North Africa - Spider - who provided him with his remaining three daughters: Intrigue, Bow, and Sea-Foam. Spider died in agonies, giving birth to Sea-Foam. And Purity has disappeared. No-one knows how she escaped or exactly when. But she didn't take her four daughters. *Is she still alive?*

But All-Gifted draws me away from my thoughts by turning to the littlest ones and raising her voice. "Hear me, sisters, especially the youngest. You have all of your life before you. If you wish to have a life, you must leave this castle. The time has come."

She taps her stick, and a shadowy hole appears beneath the rock.

I make my way to the front and follow All-Gifted, the others coming behind. The stairs twist down, and then up again. After an interminable time, we come to the top and open the door.

There is our room, in the top of the tower, just as we'd left it.

Protectress strides forward. "What kind of trick is this?"

Intrigue laughs as she glances at herself in the mirror. "So much for your power, All-Gifted. I will spend the rest of the evening with Father." She snaps her fingers, and a hovering maid clothes her in yet another jewel-encrusted robe, rearranges her hair, and covers it with a silken veil held in place by a circlet of gold. The door bangs shut as she sweeps out.

"A fine sorceress you are!" Protectress seats herself on her bed with a snort. "Don't stand there, staring," she snaps at the maid. "Help me to bed."

"We'll never get out now," Death-Bringer sinks onto her bed, hiding her face in her hands.

All-Gifted droops over her cauldron, her face slack with despair. "My spells are not strong enough," she mutters.

And that is the last time I hear her speak for quite a while.

FIVE

The Princess with Intelligent Eyes

Playful speaks

The sun's glare prevents me from seeing much until I sidle inside, into the cool humid air of several horses' breaths.

"I saw them!" I exclaim.

Father tilts his head up. It is so dark in the gloom of the stables that the only things visible are his cool silvery eyes. He is seated against a haystack, mending something.

"Who?"

"The twelve mysterious princesses."

Father barks out a laugh. "You mean the twelve cursed sisters."

My excitement vanishes as I take a seat beside him.

For the first time, the fact of their imprisonment strikes home. I cannot imagine being forbidden to go outside, being prevented from having the company of friends. Most of all, I could not imagine foregoing the freedom to come and go as I please. I would go mad if I were confined. These women are like caged beasts. They exist in an accursed tomb.

"So, you saw them?" prompts Father.

"Yes. They were on Ceres rock. Just outside the castle walls."

"How did they get there?"

"I don't know."

It had been a beautiful autumnal night in late September, the moon blazing in the sky. I'd breathed in the sweet air as the door banged shut, closing off the dank confines of the smelly hall, a mixture of sweaty bodies, spilled beer, and piss.

Slowly, I made my way to Ceres rock, a holy place for Demeter, goddess of fertility and grain.

As I near the rocky outcropping that juts up in full view of the castle, shadowy forms appear, wreathed in silken robes that shimmer in the light breeze. These beings have high voices and long hair. They are priestesses come to pay tribute to the goddess. I crouch down.

"Where are we?" asks a high voice.

"Are we going to die?" squeaks an even higher voice.

Not priestesses then. I peer up, counting them. They are twelve.

"It's too cold out here," says one of the larger figures. "I'm going back for my cloak."

"What are we going to do when Father finds out?"

So. These must be the famous princesses. But why are they here? Shouldn't they be locked in their tower?

Another figure with a stick points a finger at them.

They freeze mid-motion.

I still. Tentatively I flex my fingers. They work.

Slowly, oh-so-slowly, I crawl backward, setting off a skitter of pebbles that bounce down the rocky slope.

I hold my breath, hunched amidst a stand of olive trees.

What was that raucous song the men were singing the other night? Let's see. The figure with the stick must be the Sorceress, the eldest daughter. Only she would have the power to freeze people.

"What are you going to do?" asks one. This blonde-haired blue-eyed beauty tilts her chin, revealing a well-cut profile with high cheekbones.

The woman with the stick, who must be Lady All-Gifted the eldest princess, climbs to the top of the rock. "I am going to set you free," she replies. "Do you want to be like me? Do you want to spend the best years of your life moldering away in a tower, waiting for the prince that never comes?"

"Father has a brilliant marriage planned for me!" exclaims the beauty.

"Hmm." Father leans forward. "That must be Lady Intrigue."

"What a name," I say.

"Lady Intrigue is the King's favorite daughter." He looks at me as if he would say more, but shakes his head and turns away.

"How old is she?"

"Fifteen."

"Oh. Then that makes the eldest thirty, for I heard her say she was twice Intrigue's age."

Father nods. "Lady All-Gifted has thirty years."

"She is only a little younger than you Father."

Father nods absently. I know how much he misses Mother, but he hasn't seen her for over ten years. But are the rumors true? That Father has met and married many women in his years away from Mother?

"Was there anyone else?" Father's voice pulls me out of my thoughts.

"Yes, the one I told you about before. She's not a beauty like Intrigue, but she has a lovely pear-shaped face. I think you would like her, Father."

His gaze bores into me. "Why do you say that?"

"I don't know." I fumble for my purse. "She left this behind."

Father takes the grey ribbon and inhales its scent.

"Her eyes are grey." It is a statement, not a question.

"Yes," I reply, grasping at a thread of thought. "There is something special about her. Her eyes are intelligent, like yours, Father. And she was the one who first confronted Intrigue when she claimed the King had promised her a brilliant match."

He looks up. "What did she say?"

"She asked who the suitor was."

"And what did Intrigue say?"

"She didn't reply."

"Ah!" Father relaxes back against his stack of hay.

"What does it mean?"

"It means that either she has no suitor. Or she cannot name who the real suitor is."

"Why not?"

Father gets to his feet and peers out of the barn. "The sun is beginning to set," he remarks. "Time to go back to the castle."

I nod and get to my feet. When Father doesn't wish to answer a question, no amount of cajoling will make him. And whining only makes him angry.

We walk together through the bronze fields and reach the castle just as the sun begins to dip below the horizon. There is the tower, and as usual, the window is latched open.

As Father approaches, the confrontational princess with the pear-shaped face leans out to close the window. But instead of closing it, she turns her head taking in the loveliness of a cool autumnal evening.

I hear Father draw breath. I turn and look up at him.

He is staring—at her. At the princess with the intelligent eyes. She must sense something for she turns, and their eyes meet.

Her mouth relaxes into a lusciousness of full lips, and this time Father actually gasps.

Does she hear something? For her eyes widen. Then, blushing, she bangs the window shut.

I stare. At the suddenly shut window, at the absence of her presence, but most of all at Father. For his cheeks are stained a deep wine-red. I have never seen a grown man blush before. I have never seen Father look so discomforted. What is going on?

SIX~

PROTECTRESS SEEKS ADVICE

Justice speaks

A week or so passes in ominous calm as if everything is holding its breath. Then Protectress suddenly appears one evening, as I sit idly daydreaming in my window embrasure, gazing at the nearly-full moon rising in the East.

"Death-Bringer!" calls Protectress in a loud hiss.

There is no answer.

"Death-Bringer!" hisses Protectress moving towards the loom. "Are you there?" She waves a hand in front of her sister's face.

Death-Bringer slowly unbends, looking more like the young woman she is as her shuttle clatters to the floor.

"Huh?" she queries.

"We must do something about All-Gifted."

Death-Bringer looks up. "Don't you mean Intrigue?"

Protectress arranges herself on her bed, tucking the folds of her robe around her. Like All-Gifted, Protectress has an unfortunate name. She is no protectress but a cauldron of simmering rage with not an ounce of kindness. She wears robes of varying shades of white, edged in dull red, the color of dried blood. But it is her hair that causes the greatest alarm to those who don't know her. For her thick plaits are actually snakes, writhing against her head.

Something happened while All-Gifted and I were away at that Bride Show, where All-Gifted was supposed to marry Prince Lover-of-God and become the next Empress of Constantinople. Something no one will ever say out loud in public, not the lowliest servant, not the shepherd boy, not the farmers who come from the countryside to sell the goodness of their orchards and farms. Circulating gossip provided in thread-like whispers says that Athena is punishing Protectress for doing something unthinkable. In her temple. But once, in an unguarded moment, Protectress declared she was being punished for something Death-Bringer had done. So why isn't she furious with Death-Bringer? Instead, her anger-beyond-rage is directed at Father. Perhaps it is because Death-Bringer is so broken. Death-Bringer never smiles. Death-Bringer, like All-Gifted, has grown old before her time.

Now, the snakes hiss invitingly, as Protectress pats the seat beside her.

Death-Bringer rises from her stool and carefully sits down next to her sister, just out of range of the snakes. She wraps her light-green wraith-like cloak around her as her blank hazel eyes slowly come to life.

I shrink into my favorite place in the window embrasure, folding my piece of embroidery out of sight. I wait, cocking an ear, for Death-Bringer is soft-spoken.

"Tell me," says Protectress in her hissy voice, "why you think Intrigue is a problem."

Death-Bringer focuses her eyes on her sister. "She is Father's favorite," she replies slowly. "Now that Purity has gone, she has taken her place as Lady of this house. The place is yours, Protectress, by right."

Protectress languidly waves a hand. "Intrigue is no longer a problem." She pauses and looks around the room, but fails to see me, curled up in my grey robes in the stone embrasure, grey on grey.

"Intrigue is expecting a baby."

Death-Bringer stares at her sister. "How?"

Protectress sighs and pats her hand. The snakes give an accompanying hiss. "You of all people should know."

Death-Bringer sags in her seat, putting her head in her hands. As she does so, strands of memory begin to weave together. Many blame All-Gifted for our predicament. But then All-Gifted tends to be blamed for everything that has gone wrong. However, it must have been Death-Bringer who brought dishonor to our family. Did she have a baby? If so, who was her paramour? And where is he now?

"I need your help," continues Protectress.

Death-Bringer turns away, but Protectress grabs her wrist.

"Listen!" she hisses. "Father is never going to let us go. If we don't make our own escape we'll sit here until death takes us."

"I am already dead," murmurs Death-Bringer.

"You may not care, but what about me? All-Gifted's silly spells don't work."

"You're the second daughter. Everyone thinks All-Gifted mad, except for Justice," says Death-Bringer.

"Justice? Don't talk to me about that whey-faced fool!" snaps Protectress.

I flinch and sink deeper into the shadows.

"No one thinks All-Gifted suitable," continues Death-Bringer. "She may be the eldest daughter, but she never does anything to help Father. You have to act as hostess when he's entertaining foreign princes and diplomats."

"True," Protectress bites her lip. "But he doesn't treat me like his heiress."

Maybe the snakes are a problem, I murmur to myself. Protectress has tried many times to take All-Gifted's place and become lady of the land. Unfortunately, few like her. The last time she tried, Father shut her up in one of his dungeons for a month, to the applause of his men. It has been many a long year since she's gathered the courage to plot again. Now, she is being more careful by seeking Death-Bringer's advice.

Death-Bringer rises. "Why do you need my help, Protectress? Why don't you go to Father?"

Protectress searches Death-Bringer's face for a long moment but sees nothing but her usual weary expression. She casts her eyes down. "He never listens to me," she mutters.

"Talk to All-Gifted, then."

"So, you won't help?"

"You don't need me." Death-Bringer moves back to her stool and hunches over her loom. The click of the shuttle and the whisper of thread start up again. I peer out into the smoky darkness that hovers over the keep as afternoon melts into evening. How Death-Bringer can see to weave, I have no idea.

Protectress crumples onto her bed, suddenly old and tired. Then, she bites her lip, smiles, and leaves.

I straighten up, stretching my cramped limbs.

Death-Bringer continues weaving. "You heard." It was quiet, without challenge.

"Indeed, I did. What's got into Protectress?"

"A soldier has arrived."

"What is his name?"

"I don't know. He calls himself Nobody, but that is obviously a cloak to hide who he really is." She looks up at me as a rare smile appears on her face. "But he carries himself well. He could be a prince—or perhaps a king."

I roll my eyes. "A knight in shining armor who will rescue us from Father's dungeon." I pause. "Except that Protectress will take him for herself."

"Protectress will want him as her suitor," agrees Death-Bringer, her voice softening into its usual dreaminess.

"She wants to stop All-Gifted," I murmur. "She doesn't trust All-Gifted to carry out her plan of freeing all of us, either because she doesn't think she's got the power, or because she doesn't believe All-Gifted will free *her*. They don't get along."

Death-Bringer shoots me a look. "Maybe she should worry more about *you*. This soldier seems sweet on you."

I recoil, trying to forget a pair of silvery eyes looking up at me. "What do you mean? No one notices me."

"He says he's seen you sitting by the window."

"He must have uncommonly good eyesight," I retort, picking up my embroidery. Then I pause. I don't like that smile on Protectress's face. Where has she gone? What is she doing now?

SEVEN~

SHINING THE NAUGHTY

Justice continues her story

I can hear Protectress's distinctive voice before I see her. "Shining," she says somewhere between a hiss and a spit, "Get up! I have something important to say to you."

I descend the stairs into the gardens that surround our tower. We are allowed this small measure of freedom because Father's physicians insist on our having a daily dose of fresh air and exercise. The last time Father forbade us to leave our Tower-Prison, nearly all of us came down with a sweating sickness. Even Father saw that it wouldn't look good if his daughters died. And so, he reluctantly agreed to the dictates of his physicians.

As I move further into the gardens, I see twenty-three-year-old Shining draped artfully alongside the pool, her white diaphanous dress swirling around her ankles in the soft afternoon breeze, her long, waist-length golden hair tumbled around her head and shoulders.

The guards, because there are always guards, lounge around, grinning as they take up positions that give them the best view of her breasts and legs. As Protectress approaches, they snap to attention, their gaze never flickering over to the snakes.

Shining's eyes are closed showing perfectly made-up lids with little flourishes at the outer corners of each eye, where the upper and lower lids meet. As Protectress looms over her, Shining's lids lift slowly, oh-so-slooowly. Her eyes are unusual, deep green with an amber fleck in her left eye. She truly is the most beautiful woman in the world, a magnet for the male eye.

"What now?" she yawns.

"I need your help," hisses Protectress

"*My* help?" Shining rolls to a kneel and peers up at her sister. "You never come to me for anything."

"Is it any wonder?" snaps Protectress gesturing at the guards.

Shining sighs as she rises to her feet. "You have *no idea* how tiresome it is to be the most beautiful woman in the world."

Protectress stares at her. "What?"

"I am trapped," remarks Shining, "by the male stare."

Protectress does something she never does. She laughs, in great gulping gasps. The snakes uncoil, hissing loudly.

"I need your help," she repeats, wiping her eyes. "If we don't exert ourselves, we'll never get out of here."

Shining looks around her. "What else is there?"

"Life," says Protectress

"My life is a *golden cage,*" remarks Shining settling herself by the pool again. She crosses one pretty foot over the other. "Don't you remember what that fortune teller said when I was only seven? That men would start a great war over me?" She yawns like a cat. "I am destined to be a *pawn* in the affairs of men."

"Don't you want power for yourself?" I remark coming forward.

"What power? Women like me never have any. We are just possessions, pretty toys to play with and be discarded."

"Are you following me around?" Protectress steps in too close, the snakes' forked tongues reaching out to lick my face.

I hastily step backward and lift my chin. "I find your company fascinating, dear sister." I brace myself for the blow I know is coming, when twenty-one-year-old Maiden appears, her basket full of her usual things, jars full of ointments, surrounded by bandages, scissors, and various small knives. She settles down next to Shining and begins the tedious task of rolling bandages.

"Why don't you help?" she remarks, staring at Shining's supine form, arranged into another alluring pose alongside the pool.

Shining's lids lift briefly. "What for? There's no point to anything. We're just going to grow old and become dust."

"You could make your own purpose," remarks Maiden. "You could use your talents to help others."

"And become a doctor like you, I suppose."

"Why not? It's better than being a decoration. What's going to happen when you wrinkle up and go grey? You owe yourself more than that."

"I'll be dead by then," murmurs Shining closing her eyes.

"If you're so extraordinary, why don't *you* help?" hisses Protectress.

"Me?" says Maiden. "What makes you think Father will listen to me? He probably doesn't even know I exist. He has so many daughters, he can only keep track of the four eldest: All-Gifted, you Protectress, Death-Bringer, and Shining. I am the fifth daughter, so I am forgettable."

"I am forgettable too," remarks a soft voice, as a shadowy form emerges from the olive trees that surround the garden.

"You're not forgettable, you're invisible!" retorts Protectress.

Morgana, the Great Sorceress employed by Father to teach us magic, gave us each a special power.

To Shadow, she gave the Power of Disappearing.

To Maiden, the Power of Healing.

To Shining, the Power of Beauty.

To Death-Bringer the Power of Peace-Weaving.

To Protectress the Power, or some would say the Curse, of Ambition.

To All-Gifted, she gave the Power of The Glamor, of taking on the guise of another.

And to me, Justice, she gave the Power of Bravery.

Shadow flinches but doesn't reply. She is never without her drop spindle which she now drops from her hand and twirls before winding the new thread onto the shaft. Drop, twirl, wind. Drop, twirl, wind.

"What about you?" Protectress turns to her.

Shadow freezes. "Me?"

"Yes, you. You are the sixth daughter. Why don't *you* do something useful for once? Come with me to persuade Father to let us go!"

"But—but—" she stammers, her thread unwinding as the spindle bobs near her feet.

"Why are you bullying her?" I come forward. "Of course, she does something useful. Shadow is our best spinner. Every minute of every day she spins the evenest and smoothest thread of us all. Without her, we wouldn't have our clothes, our fine linens, or our woolen blankets to keep us warm."

"She's no use to me!" snaps Protectress. "Father is never going to listen to—Her Shyness."

I fold my arms. "Your plan makes little sense Protectress. You know Father is not going to listen to any of us. He enjoys locking us up and stealing our lives."

"Do you have a better plan?"

"Yes. I do. I think it is highly risky, not to say foolhardy to go to Father at all. You know what he's like when he's in one of his rages. Do you really want him to know that we're actually thinking of escaping?"

"No. It's much better he doesn't know," says Maiden.

Shining opens her eyes. "Go on," she says.

"We need to get Father's attention," I say. "And the best way of doing that is by making him worry. If something strange were to happen to us—"

"Something strange has already happened to All-Gifted," mutters Protectress.

I turn to her. "It has to happen to all of us Protectress, to make him care. He doesn't care about All-Gifted at all. He's spent the last ten years watching her sink into madness, without lifting a hand to help her."

"Sooo," hisses Protectress. "We need something that would really unsettle Father." She smiles slowly, showing her teeth.

EIGHT~

THE MYSTERIOUS SUITOR

Justice continues her story

Thoughtfully I walk up those twisting stairs to that large round room all twelve of us call home. As I cross the threshold, something moves.

I lift my head and tense.

"Death-Bringer?" I call.

Silence. But that is not unusual, for Death-Bringer is usually in a trance as she weaves her wool. A shadow detaches itself from the curtains that surround Intrigue's bed, and the man with the silvery eyes appears.

I freeze, in shock. What is a fully-grown man doing in our *bedroom*?

Up close, he is not particularly good-looking, a muscular man of middling height, with a barrel chest and reddish hair that is beginning to grey around the temples. But his eyes draw me in. They are grey, but not the soft greyness of river mist at dawn. They are hard and bright, radiating energy like two silver discs, lodestones, compelling my attention.

"Who are you?" I snap.

He bows. "Lady Justice."

How does he know my name? I turn to escape, but he blocks the way to the stairs.

"I have been waiting for over an hour to see you."

"Don't be ridiculous," I snap again. But my cheeks warm. Gracious Goddess!

He puts his hand on my arm and a blessed calm washes over me. Once I gaze up into his eyes, he speaks again. "We have met before, my lady. Don't you remember?"

Various tart replies come to mind, but strangely, I find myself unable to speak.

His eyes soften. "I saw your lovely face in the window and became intrigued." He bends and kisses my hand. "I desired to meet you in person."

His voice, honey-sweet, lingers over the word *desired*. My heart bounces in my chest like a child's ball. I stiffen. He is playing me like a lyre. I lift my chin.

"What are you talking about?" I say, my voice hard and angry. "You shouldn't be here. This is our private chamber. If Father knew of this, he would punish you most severely."

He smirks. "You mean he comes here *in person* every day to satisfy himself that *all* of his lovely daughters are behaving themselves?"

I consider this question and decide not to answer. This stranger presumes too much.

"Well, then," he smiles. "Please." He gestures to the nearest chair, inviting me to sit as if I am in his private room.

For the first time, I notice his clothes. When I'd seen him before, he'd been dressed as a rough peasant. Now, he wears Kingly garb, a fine woolen tunic with embroidery around the hem, long boots of the softest leather, and even a circlet on his head. Who is this arrogant man? And where is the boy he was with?

I glare at him. "But my sisters come up here."

"At what time?"

Ignoring him, I move further into the room.

"When the sun slips into the sea," comes Death-Bringer's dreamy voice, "to get ready for supper."

He smiles and bows. "Lady Death-Bringer." He turns back to me. "By my reckoning, Lady Justice, we have an hour."

Death-Bringer rises, her smile easing the care-lines off her face. I draw in my breath. My sister is indeed beautiful, but she has the unearthly beauty of a wood sprite, her clothes the palest green of early spring. I can almost see her standing in a grove of trees in the cold sun of early morning, a basket of freshly-picked flowers at her side. That is how she used to be, before she was abducted.

"We are glad of your company, my lord. What news do you bring from the outside world?"

He shrugs and turns to me. "More of the same. Wars, famine, people divided, people brought together, death, birth, marriage."

"Are there any bride shows?" I ask.

"No, nor like to be soon. The Emperor is already spoken for, and his wife has just given him another son." He peers at the growing gloom of early evening. "You must be *dying* to get out of here."

Death-Bringer lowers her head and sinks onto her stool, old and dusty yet again. "I will never get out," she murmurs.

"Why not? Are you doing penance?"

She turns to her loom.

"Is that why you're here?" I ask. "To get us out?"

"I will do anything you wish, my lady."

I study him. He must be about twenty years younger than Father, so it is no surprise he is much more muscular. But there are scars everywhere, on his arms, his face, and his legs. Has he been in a war? Somehow the scars on his face are not disfiguring, only increasing the interest of an older face. He has a lithe strength that belies his barrel chest. Quick on his feet, he blocked the way to the stairs with lightning speed to prevent me from escaping. But is he good with a sword? Or with bow and arrow? And more to the point, is he more likely to get us out of here than either All-Gifted or Protectress?

"Too dangerous," I say.

"Not if done right," he replies, meeting my stare. He smiles, making his grey eyes sparkle. I sense a fierce intelligence there. Immediately, I lean in, dying to hear more.

"The first thing is to make your father worry."

"I know," I say. "But how?"

He bows again and takes my hand. "Suppose one of you were to marry—"

"You, I suppose," I put in.

His eyes light. Then he flushes and coughs.

"Or escape," says Death-Bringer. "You could help us with that, my lord."

He bows. "The best plan for escaping is to throw your father off guard. And the best way of doing that is for you ladies to do something strange, or unusual."

Death-Bringer raises her sad face. "He'd just stop us from going outside at all. At least I can see the stars, during the nights when I cannot sleep." Her voice trails off.

He takes my hand as if leading me to dance. "Now is the time to transform—your lives."

I stare at him. Why is he saying that? Has he seen us on Ceres rock?

"Your father would worry if you did something that would affect your marriageability," he continues.

Death-Bringer flushes and turns away.

Clearly, he must be newly-arrived not to realize the problems my elder sisters face. What with All-Gifted's madness, Protectress's hair writhing with snakes, Death-Bringer's grief (not to mention her strange name), Shining's too-overt sexuality, Maiden's tart tongue, and Shadow's crippling shyness, no sensible man would want my sisters as wives.

"And it must be something that happens to you all."

"I don't like your suggestions," I remark, wrenching my hand away from his. "They are not seemly. You should remember that you are talking to the King's daughters. Surely you cannot believe we would do anything to ruin our reputations?"

His eyes become flints of steel as he bows too low.

"Of course not, my lady." He moves towards the door. "Glory to the House of the Silver-Tongued." His voice has a sarcastic edge.

"What is your name?"

"Nobody," he replies. Then he vanishes.

Goose-bumps spread all over my arms. How does he know so much about us?

As I fall asleep that night, I feel as if I am falling into a sea of grey. Slowly, the mists clear and there are two disks of light beckoning me forward.

"How do you know so much?" I whisper.

"My Power lies in Divining Secrets." His voice echoes, as if we are in an underground cave, no, a tunnel, a dark tunnel with a rushing stream that ends in a pool of silver. The water is unnaturally calm, death-like.

"People seem like tranquil pools," he murmurs into my ear. "But they are not. The trick is to plunge down to the bottom and recover their secrets."

"But how?"

His laughter echoes around and around until it dies down, becoming whispery, like the sound of dead leaves scattered by a passing breeze.

NINE

THE BRIDE SHOW

Justice continues her story

I toss and turn all night. Damn him, I mutter to myself. Why cannot I get those grey eyes out of my thoughts? Why does he trouble me so much? I won't marry for many a long year, if at all, for I have six older sisters looking for a husband. In any case, I don't want a husband, I want to be free. As free as one of Father's falcons when their hoods and jesses are slipped, and they soar high into the air. And he is old, so old, he must be *twice* my age. So why do I spend endless amounts of time thinking about him? Who wants the humiliation and shame of being tupped by a man, followed by the messy and often fatal process of birthing a child? And why would I want to marry after what happened to All-Gifted at that Bride Show? I close my eyes as memories swirl.

Ten years ago, All-Gifted was a normal young woman like us. Indeed, her unusual beauty, her red-gold hair, blue-green eyes, and velvet skin the color of mare's milk, led everyone to expect her to become the next Empress. For Emperor Gift-of-God, the second of that name, had recently died and his sixteen-year-old son Prince Lover-of-God had succeeded to the throne.

Father immediately sent messengers to inquire when the Bride Show was to take place, and received a personal invitation from Lady Merry, the stepmother of the prince, inviting him to send his most beautiful daughter. Naturally, he picked his eldest daughter, twenty-year-old All-Gifted. And so, once mud season passed, All-Gifted set out for Constantinople, Queen of Cities. It was a glorious spring day when the rising sun warmed the new leaves veiling the trees.

I was sent along to help, as, at six, I had perfected the art of embroidering songbirds, roses, and curlicues in gold thread, silver thread, or any deep-dyed color of silk that one could find. My task was to help All-Gifted's women keep her finery in good order. I spent the entire journey helping to create another robe, in case that green satin one which fell like a waterfall from her strong, well-shaped shoulders, should be damaged by a careless spill of wine, a splash from a wave, or some other misfortune.

All-Gifted's retinue, guarded by a large party of knights, included many ladies, most of them bringing their daughters. I did not know them, for they lived in the outlying valleys away from our castle. Why Father agreed to let them go with us was a mystery to me. Perhaps he thought we would like the company, for, of All-Gifted's sisters, I was the only one present, the others being left behind with Father. But then, my eldest sister always had a special fondness for me.

There was one other person whom I knew, and that was Morgana, the great sorceress whom Father employed to train All-Gifted in herbal lore, in the patient distillation of plants and roots into elixirs and tonics, to help people bear the toils of this life. That first day, Morgana announced to all and sundry that she was traveling to Constantinople to act as my sister's chief woman and chaperone. It did not take long for some to whisper that the real reason she was coming was to brew a love potion. For why else would the King part with his great sorceress?

I had never heard of a Bride Show, but my companions assured me that all emperors of the Eastern Roman Empire now held them as a means of finding a wife.

"It doesn't seem right to me," said one prune-faced dame as we cantered East to the sea. "Borrowing a custom from those heathen tribes of the Steppes. But the Emperor is now great friends with them. What is their name?"

"Khazars," replied a young woman with hair the color of ice, who cantered next to her, a puff of un-spun wool peeking out from her saddlebags.

"But why would he be friends with Barbarians?" I asked.

"My husband tells me they can shoot to kill from a distance of several feet, twisting in the saddle and galloping off thereafter so they can't be caught. The Emperor has decided he'd rather have those Turkish horse-archers fighting for him, than against him."

I shivered, imagining a band of horse-archers appearing over the horizon, their bows pointed straight at me. But I was a big girl now and mustn't show how unsettled I was. I straightened my shoulders, sitting tall in my seat, causing the guard I was riding pillion with to grunt as he shifted to make room for me.

I had no idea Constantinople was so far away from our home in the mountains of Eastern Sikelia. That day, we rode down to the port which lay below the flanks of our cloud-breathing mountain of fire and took ship. As the coastline receded, all there was to show of our home was that mountain, whom some call Mount Aitna, curled up like a goddess in sleep, a sulky spill of cloud emanating from her peak. It was March when we left, for Father's astrologer had predicted it would take two full turnings of the moon for us to reach our destination.

We sailed East, past the southern shores of a land that stretched north to our mother home of Eliada, which had founded many colonies on our shores thousands of years before. In fact, the language my family spoke together was a kind of Greek, though some of the others, Intrigue especially, delighted in chattering away in Arabic, a language they'd no doubt learned from those slaves who'd come from Africa. Finally, we passed Eliada and sailed north-east to the Bosporus, to that jut of land where Europe touches Asia, where Constantinople, Queen of Cities lay.

It was magnificent. I had never been to a city before and could not imagine where all those people lived. Where did they sleep at night? Did they have houses? How could it be possible for there to be so many houses in one place?

I was pulled out of my thoughts by All-Gifted, who wanted me to hold her mirror for her.

"He's sure to choose you, my lady." The cold grey sky gleamed silver as the day of the Bride Show dawned. Morgana brushed All-Gifted's red tresses until they gleamed a burnished copper in the light of the rising sun that flooded the chamber.

"If nothing else, he'll fall in love with the color of your eyes."

All-Gifted squinted into the mirror. Her eyes were a kind of speckled green, like certain kinds of amber I'd seen in the great market of Constantinople, being peddled by tall northerners with yellow hair and chilly blue eyes. Some people referred to All-Gifted's unusual eyes as cat's eyes, and perhaps they were the reason why All-Gifted had no suitors, even though she was now twenty years old. This Bride Show would be her last chance.

She stood and held out her arms, allowing Morgana to put her robe over her head. The satin-green robe, chosen to match those eyes, was thick with golden embroidery woven here and there with glints of coppery thread, which matched the color of her hair. I had embroidered that gown myself, with the help of a person who'd been employed by Father to teach me that skill. Her name was Spider, and she was a dancer from Tunisia. In time, she became Father's concubine and the mother of three of his daughters, but that is another story.

All-Gifted stood tall as she looked at herself in the sheet of polished silver Morgana had attached to the door of our chamber. She lifted her chin. Her height gave her a queenly bearing. Her hair fell in a river of amber gold under a thin circlet of reddish gold, and if she kept out of the sun there would be no lemony freckles to mar the creamy whiteness of her skin.

Morgana smiled. "You are the fairest lady of them all. If he doesn't choose you, then the god of wine must be out and about, making mischief!

As we straightened from our low curtsies, we found ourselves in a sea of people, standing around a large round room. It was obvious who the other brides were by the magnificence of their jewels. Slowly, I counted. There were eleven other brides.

"Welcome, my dear," remarked a rasping voice. I turned. This lady wore a diadem with enormous egg-shaped emeralds, the exact same color as All-Gifted's robe.

All-Gifted dipped into a deep curtsey. "Lady Merry," she murmured.

I stared at this woman who looked to be around the same age as my sister. I hadn't realized that Prince Lover-of-God had a mother who was so young. Then I remembered. She wasn't actually his mother, but his stepmother, Emperor Gift-of-God's second or third or perhaps even his fourth wife.

But Lady Merry was not smiling at my sister." I thought you already married," she remarked.

All-Gifted flushed.

"For one with such regal beauty, that surprises me. So, you are interested in my son?"

All-Gifted stared at her. Why did she think she had come all this way, traveled one thousand miles—

"Tell me your age, dear."

"I have twenty autumns," murmured. All-Gifted.

"The prince has sixteen summers," replied Lady Merry, her voice ringing throughout that magnificent chamber. She made a gesture to a waiting scribe and moved on to the next young woman, a diminutive girl with bland blue eyes and pale fair hair.

Lady Merry spent a long time with her, a Lady Theodora from somewhere to the East. It was hard to see why, as the young lady said very little. Instead, she studied the richly-hued carpet beneath her slippered feet, while her women bobbed their heads and smiled, and an older woman talked volubly with many hand gestures.

Slowly, oh-so-slowly, Lady Merry progressed around the room, greeting each bridal candidate, talking with them at length. Some of them she seemed to know well. My stomach clenched as All-Gifted's face paled, her disappointment radiating from her in waves. But she was a princess, so she merely folded her hands, copying her rival by staring at her feet, as motionless in that heavy robe as one of those icons of Our Savior and Lord Jesus Christ and his Saints, that adorned that over-decorated room.

Eventually, Lady Merry finished her perambulation. She smiled. "The prince has made his choice."

I looked around, but the prince was nowhere to be seen. Indeed, neither All-Gifted nor the other brides had been formally introduced to him.

Lady Merry beckoned, and All-Gifted took a step forward, soon realizing her mistake. For it was the Lady Theodora, the shy, flaxen-haired young lady, who now approached, giggling nervously behind her hand.

"She's chosen Theodora of Armenia," whispered someone.

All-Gifted whirled around, swept out, and ran to her room.

We followed.

Once there, she tore her magnificent robe off, ruining it forever, and slumped to the floor. "No! No!" All-Gifted banged her fists into the marble floor. "I can't bear it! Why her? She's such a silly thing!"

"Because she is a silly thing." Morgana closed the door, picked up the torn robe, and with a sigh, tossed it into All-Gifted's chest.

"But I'm more suitable!" All-Gifted tore at her hair with her nails, rending her silken veil, causing her hair to fall free. "I'm well-educated, I can read, and I know herbal lore —"

"You're too well-educated, my lady. Lady Merry wanted a malleable young woman as her son's wife."

"Why didn't you tell me that before? It would have saved me a great deal of trouble. Not to mention the expense this journey has cost us."

"How was I to know, my lady?"

All-Gifted slapped her hard across the cheek. "You never give me advice at the right time! You claim to be able to see into the future, but it doesn't help anyone! You let Mother die before her time—"

"My lady, that is not fair!" Morgana poured a salve onto a napkin and held it against her cheek. "I was devoted to Lady Beauty. I had no idea your father had eyes for that sly-faced nun. How was I to know he would arrange matters—

"So that Mother was cold in her grave before the year was out? What's the point of being a sorceress if you don't know these things?"

"Some things are mysterious, my lady. The gods are not always kind—

"I am cursed!" All-Gifted sobbed. "I have ten younger sisters waiting to be married. Father promised me they would never marry until my own match had taken place. So, what is he going to do now? What if I never marry?"

"That is for the fates to decide."

In one swift movement, All-Gifted rose to her feet.

"Go!" she screamed. "You haven't helped me at all. Begone! I don't want to see you ever again."

And so, Morgana left, no one knew where.

All-Gifted returned home in a dark mood that never lifted, not for these ten years. Father promised her that he would never allow her sisters to marry while she remained a maiden. Then he kept his promise by locking us up.

And so, All-Gifted never married.

And now, I wonder. Did Father lock us up to save himself the considerable expense of providing those twelve piles of pure golden pieces needed for our dowries?

TEN

THE BITE

Justice continues her story

It begins with Shining. The fourth daughter of King Silver-Tongued and Lady Beauty, Shining is twenty-three years old and obsessed with clothes—and men. Yes, she behaves exactly like Intrigue, except that Intrigue wields power as Father's favorite, whereas Shining, a younger daughter of the discarded first wife, is not looked upon so favorably. Unlike Intrigue who has only to clap her pretty hands to bring the seamstress running, Shining is reduced to wearing Intrigue's castoffs.

As the twelve of us toil up those spiral stairs towards the end of another long day,

Shining stumbles as she enters our chamber. We cluster about her, but she breaks free, hopping around the room, too agitated to speak. At length, she gives an unearthly cry, falling to the floor, senseless.

We are speechless. Shining has never behaved like this before. Hopping is not something she would do by choice because the movement is not graceful or seductive enough. We bend over her, clapping our hands to awaken her, then quieting down to check for the slow rise and fall of breath, while All-Gifted declaims her spells.

The door opens a crack, and the arrogant man appears again.

Today he is dressed in hunting garb with those long, soft, leather boots sans circlet. He is followed by his boy, a pretty thing with a well-cut face, similar grey eyes, and a mop of corn-colored curls. If this is his son, where is his wife?

He arches an eyebrow.

Frowning, I rise to my feet. "What are you doing here?"

"She needs fresh air."

"We cannot move her out of this chamber and down those steep and narrow steps. We don't have the strength."

He bows. "Allow me to help."

"It is against Father's orders."

He puts his hand on my arm and looks at me, his grey eyes the color of a stormy sea. "You want your sister to get better."

"Of course."

"Well, then." He beckons and more men appear.

"This is outrageous!" I exclaim, as they surround Shining and gently roll her up into one of Father's fine carpets for her trip downstairs.

"You are more than welcome to follow," he replies with a low bow.

I turn back to the room and beckon to my sisters, who are now smiling at the men, except for All-Gifted, who is wrapped up in her spells.

"Follow me," I say sighing, taking Intrigue's arm, dragging her away from the boy, who flushes as she practices her sidelong glances on him.

My sisters traipse after me down those interminable stairs and out into the garden, where an orange-colored moon glares at us from just above the horizon. The littlest ones start to whimper, having no one to turn to with Intrigue still absorbed in embarrassing her pretty boy. And so, I ask Maiden, the most Christian princess amongst us (for she is the eldest daughter of Purity the Nun), to take charge, and sing some soothing hymns.

We set Shining on the ground and I bend over her, slapping her ankles, her arms, even her face. But nothing happens. I sit back on my heels. Should I slap her harder? Part of me longs to, partly as a way of letting out my long pent-up irritation. But I don't want to hurt her in front of a gaggle of strange men.

"She's been bitten," murmurs the arrogant man quietly.

I glare up at him. "Show me."

He bows. "I think you should find it."

I flush. "Where is it?"

"On the lady's thigh, quite high up."

I look, and there it is. I slap him hard on the cheek. "How dare you! You have no right to—"

"I didn't see it," he replies, holding his cheek.

"Don't lie to me!"

"I didn't see it, because I didn't need to. I knew it would be there."

I raise an eyebrow.

"She has been bitten by a tarantula."

I shudder. Tarantulas are enormous spiders that lurk around this land at dusk. "Will she live?"

He looks around, but my younger sisters are clustered around Maiden, who is praying, my elder sisters having left, all except for Intrigue, now sitting alone by the pool, absorbed in re-arranging her hair. He comes closer.

"*The Mysteries of Ariadne,*" he breathes into my ear.

"What?"

"And now I should leave you."

I put my hand on his arm. "I don't even know your name."

He smiles. "But you do. It is Nobody." Then he vanishes into the shadows.

"But what about Shining?" I call after him. "How do we heal her?"

Breezes stir in the trees. The silence is deafening.

ELEVEN~

AMBIGUITY

Justice continues her story

Ariadne. Eh-ree-ad-nee. I run that name across my tongue. Isn't that the name of Spider, the dancer from North Africa who gave Father three daughters: Intrigue, Bow, and Sea-Foam? She died bringing Sea-Foam into this world. Ariadne is Spider's name in Greek, and now I think about it the arrogant man who calls himself *Nobody* has a distinctive Greek accent.

Of course, we all speak Greek, Sikelia is a Greek colony. But the Greek we speak is mixed in with various native dialects. Nobody's Greek is—purer somehow. Is he from Greece? Who is he really?

I sigh in frustration. How typical of a man to give out such a useless piece of advice. It is easy for him to casually mention *The Mysteries of Ariadne* - whatever they are - when he can come and go as he pleases. But how will I ever find out about them locked up in Father's keep?

True, we are allowed to roam around the castle, but we are not allowed outside its walls. This is Father's way of controlling who we can see. Apart from my eleven sisters and Father, there is no one else to talk to. The servants could be of little use.

I sit up on my bed, drawing my knees to my chin. Is that true? Morgana, the sorceress who trained All-Gifted, was the daughter of—I frown. If memory served, Morgana appeared out of nowhere. No one knew anything about her. All this had happened before I was born, because originally, Morgana had been All-Gifted's wet nurse.

I rise from my bed and pace. I can hear the sound of giggles as my sisters walk in the garden, enjoying a cool autumnal evening. The chamber is empty. Even Death-Bringer's loom lies untouched, bright in a shaft of sunlight while All-Gifted's cauldron squats lumpy and heavy in its corner.

Where is All-Gifted? And whatever happened to Morgana? After All-Gifted dismissed her, she vanished back into the shadows from whence she came. If only I could talk to her now.

Idly, I pull at a loose thread hanging from Death-Bringer's loom. If anyone knew about the *Mysteries of Ariadne,* Morgana did. A plume of smoke softly emanates from the end of the thread, filling the air. A form gradually emerges. It looks both familiar and very, very old. An aura glimmers around it, now growing bright. Pulsating.

I take a step back. "Morgana?"

"No." The voice grates, sounding like an iron door needing oil on its hinges. "I am far older than she."

"Who are you?"

"My name is Heck-uh-tee. I am an old, old goddess. The witches of Pettalia worship me."

Hecate. I search my memory for my goddess lessons. Let's see, Hecate is worshipped in Greece as a protectress of the household. She has a sanctuary in Caria, the land All-Gifted, Morgana and I sailed by on our way to Constantinople. She is the goddess of crossroads, doors, night, light, magic, witchcraft, ghosts, necromancy, and sorcery.

My memory stirs to life, like a cherry tree turning its blossoms towards the rising sun as I hear Morgana tell me, "Hecate is more at home on the fringes than in the center of the Greek gods and goddesses. She is ambivalent and polymorphous. She straddles conventional boundaries and eludes definition."

The words tease me, tickling at a thread of memory. Why does Hecate seem so familiar?

"If you wish to find Morgana, ask Nobody," remarks Hecate in a voice that stretches back through time.

I step forward and gaze into her eyes—her eyes—her opal eyes. "What do you mean?"

But the form blurs and a petite, fine-boned girl appears. Her eyes are the color of the moon. She has a pale face and jet-black hair, which cascades down her back. Despite her youth, she holds herself very erect, exuding a shimmering power that manifests in the slight glimmer that surrounds her.

I gasp. There stands my twelve-year-old half-sister Ambiguity, Father's eleventh daughter. The third daughter born to him by Purity the Nun. Her sisters are tart-tongued Maiden who wishes to be a doctor, shy Shadow, and the baby of the family, five-year-old Treasure.

Ambiguity has always glimmered, but this is especially noticeable at night. Now, I can *feel* her aura of power.

I stare at her. Could one of my sisters actually be an ancient goddess? She must be experiencing her first blood as that is how my sisters - indeed, all women - come into their powers.

I go inward into my thoughts, considering my sisters one by one:

All-Gifted possesses the power of The Glamor, the ability to clothe herself in the form of another.

Protectress is cursed with naked, vengeful ambition.

Death-Bringer is a Peace-Weaver.

Shining is the loveliest woman in the world.

Maiden is a talented healer.

Shadow is gifted with invisibility, while I, Justice, am brave.

Intrigue is cursed with cunning and has been locked in a battle with Protectress for the past two years over who should dominate Father.

Bow is a gifted animal-whisperer.

But what about Sea-Foam? She is a young looking thirteen, and I do not think she has yet come into her powers.

Five-year-old Treasure is far too young for hers, but her sunny disposition, smiles, and laughter have given her the ability to scatter joy wherever she goes.

I draw in a deep breath. Today Ambiguity came into her powers as the goddess Hecate. It should be something to celebrate, but she stares up at me, her face as white as mare's milk. "What happened?" she whispers.

I gather her into my arms as we both shake uncontrollably. We climb into my bed and gradually slip into sleep.

TWELVE~

THE DEATH OF INTRIGUE

Justice continues her story

The moon slides across the sky. As the sun's first rays drift across the floor of our room, Ambiguity pulls away with a jolt and rises.

"Intrigue!" she cries. "She's *dead*!" She flies out of the room.

I follow Ambiguity, hurrying down the twisting stairs, almost tumbling, until we emerge into the sunshine. Ambiguity sails across the garden to a quiet corner where Intrigue lies crumpled in a heap, soaked in blood.

"She must have lost the baby," I murmur.

"Whose baby?" demands Ambiguity.

"Never mind," I say, belatedly remembering that Ambiguity is only twelve. I kneel before Intrigue and touch her cheek gently. It is still warm. I put my ear to her lips, but there is no sound of breathing. I sit back on my heels and scrutinize her. Her chest isn't rising and falling. On the contrary, she lies there, legs splayed, head at an odd angle, her neck almost folding back on itself. There is blood everywhere, soaking into my skirts.

Ambiguity retches onto the grass.

I gather her up and take her away, away from the blood, the gore, the stuff of nightmares, to the other side of the garden.

"Intrigue was up on the castle roof with Protectress," asserts Ambiguity in the thread-like voice of an old crone. "Intrigue was laughing, her hair lifting in the wind, her eyes sparkling as she told of Father's plans to marry her. But Protectress had this odd smile on her face. It was as if she wasn't listening to Intrigue at all. She didn't look jealous, the way she normally does." Ambiguity's now-ancient features twist into Protectress's sullen pout.

"Instead, she kept nodding and smiling. Just as Intrigue exclaimed *It's all over for you Protectress. Now I am Queen*— Protectress twined her fist in Intrigue's hair and threw her over the battlements." Ambiguity looks up, her eyes glassy. "I had no idea she had the strength."

I take her by the shoulders and give her a little shake. "How do you know that?" I whisper. "You weren't there."

"I saw it in a dream." Ambiguity's face crumples and she becomes my twelve-year-old sister again. "She fell through the sky," she sobs, "like an angel, her silken garments wings, her hair a-flame." Tears run down her face.

I take her hand, leading her towards the infirmary. As I mount the steps, a shadow crosses my line of vision. I look up to see the arrogant man staring down at me. His face is somber as he takes in my ruined clothes.

"What is your father going to do?" As usual, he already knows.

I stiffen. Father is famous for his rages. What will he do when he finds out his favorite daughter has been murdered?

"An accident?" he suggests.

I say nothing.

"It *wasn't* an accident," Ambiguity remarks too loudly.

He holds up a hand. "Lady Ambiguity," he remarks softly, "do *you* want to tell your father that?"

She stares at the ground.

"Your father is like a hawk," he remarks. "He preys on young, juicy tidbits."

She looks up at him, her eyes huge.

"You are the eleventh daughter, are you not?"

She nods.

"Forgettable."

Her mouth tightens into a line.

He bends towards her. "Best to keep it that way, don't you think?"

"Ambiguity!" Thirteen-year-old Sea Foam rushes down the steps with fourteen-year-old Bow. "Where've you been? We've already broken our fast!"

He puts a hand on Ambiguity's shoulder. "Be forgettable," he says, his voice low.

She nods and disappears with her sisters.

There is a pause as I take in the beauty of a crisp autumnal morning. The flowers display their petals for the rising sun. A bird trills out an arpeggio. A fresh breeze tangles my hair, bringing with it the metallic odor of blood, and the sweet smell of Intrigue's flesh that is already beginning to decay as the rising sun heats the air.

He takes my hand. "Come, I have something for you."

I stare up at him. "But what about Intrigue?"

"Best if others find her."

He leads me past the infirmary, out into the stables. On the back of a donkey, is a large shapeless object. He unties it with deft, quick, movements, revealing a rough canvas sack.

"That is for *me*?" I cannot keep the sarcasm from my tone.

He flushes, with anger or embarrassment, I cannot tell, undoing the string that ties it together, until something slithers out.

I jump back. Writhing snakes. No, dullish grey snakeskins. No, yards and yards of thread, the dullish grey of homespun. But when I look more closely there is a faint glimmer pulsating within.

"Wait until the waxing crescent of the moon, then spin it," he breathes in a whisper. "Wait until the moon is full, then weave it. Wait until the sickle moon hangs low, then embroider it."

"But how?" I stutter. "Why?"

"You will know," he replies.

Then he mounts the donkey and disappears down the lane.

I stand there, the shapeless sack dragging on the ground, and stare after him. How will I know?

I sigh and make for the castle tower. How am I going to get this heavy, ungainly sack up those twisting stairs? But it is surprisingly light as I lift it into my arms. It seems to shrink as I traipse up those twisting stairs so that by the time I arrive in our circular room, and my sisters lift their heads in greeting, it is small enough to tuck under one arm and hide behind my pillows.

THIRTEEN~

THE FIRST EXECUTION

Justice continues her story

While I wait for the moon to fade, before reappearing as a thin sliver of a crescent, my signal that I can begin spinning the mysterious yarn Nobody gave me, I spend hours in the Infirmary. For a death-like sleep sinks its claws into Shining, and no matter what I or Maiden or Ambiguity do, we cannot wake her up.

She would have died of starvation, had not that arrogant man who calls himself *Nobody* found a way of introducing nourishment into her body, through a hole in her arm. None of us have ever seen the like before, but Nobody assures us that it works, providing the arm does not become infected.

My sisters and I spend almost all of our time in the infirmary. On the seventh day, the noise of banging jolts us awake. We run to the window, everyone standing on my bed. There, in the corner of the garden where I found Intrigue, a wooden frame is being erected. I have never seen anything like it before. They bang away at it until dusk, when a young boy, who cannot be more than Intrigue's age is led forward, a rope tied around his neck.

I peer at him. Is this Playful? No. I have never seen him before.

He is dressed in the uniform of a recruit, so he must be new, as I know all the soldiers in the palace. He is as thin as a skeleton, which means his family must have petitioned Father for the position, because army recruits are paid enough money to keep their families back home. He looks around, blinking, as if this is the first time he has seen daylight in a while. Silently, the Sergeant-at-Arms ties his arms and legs, and withdraws a whip from the folds of his tunic.

CRACK! The whip opens a long wound that oozes blood.

The boy shrieks.

CRACK! CRACK!

The boy's shrieks rise to a scream. He pulls against the leather thongs that bind him, but they are too securely fastened.

CRACK! CRACK! CRACK!

I continue counting. The Sergeant flogs him fifteen times, for each year of Intrigue's life. By the time he is finished, there are fifteen huge welts striping his back. There is so much blood, the ground beneath his feet is slick with it.

By this time, a huge crowd has formed and I recognize many faces. I see our chamber maids, our cooks, the boys who run errands, the men who tend the garden, the fields, the animals.

Father arrives and sits on his throne, set on yet another high platform to give him the best view. The Sergeant-at-Arms waits for his signal and then pulls the boy towards the wooden frame. But the boy pulls back, with much more strength than I would have imagined after that beating.

"It wasn't me; it wasn't me!" he shouts. "I found her; I didn't kill her!"

It takes three soldiers to drag his squirming, screaming form up those stairs and attach him to the wooden frame by the rope around his neck.

Finally, they march down and take their positions around the structure.

The Sergeant-at-Arms looks at Father, who nods his head. Suddenly, a door opens beneath the boy's feet. Is this one of All-Gifted's spells? For the door tilts on its hinges, just like the door she conjured beneath her bed.

The crowd gasps as his screams suddenly cut off.

His body jerks.

Once.

Twice.

Thrice.

An eerie silence descends as his body twists in the wind.

Who is this boy? Why has Father executed him? I know he has done nothing wrong. Waves of guilt wash over me. If only I hadn't listened to Nobody. If only I had reported this to Father myself. *But what would Father have done?* says the voice in my head? *Would he have executed you instead?*

Our Father the King rises from his throne. "Thus do all miscreants meet their end!" he roars into the deafening silence. "Thus is the devil responsible for the horrific murder of my well-beloved daughter Intrigue punished! I will not tolerate any insubordination. You will obey each and every order I make. Immediately!"

The people scramble to bow their heads and kneel in the bloodied dirt.

Beside me, Ambiguity throws up on my slippers. By the time I get her to the infirmary, the crowd has dispersed and Father is alone in the garden. It is easy to see why he is alone, for he is wailing like a fatally gored boar, shouting Intrigue's name over and over again.

FOURTEEN~

THE ABDUCTION OF DEATH-BRINGER

Justice continues her story

Three nights pass, then the invisible moon turns into a crescent, a faint fingernail of light. Silently, I rise from my bed, my glimmering bundle under one arm, my drop spindle in my hand, my feet whispering down those stairs so as not to disturb my slumbering sisters. Although the instructions don't say so, I feel a powerful need to do this work at night, and in secret.

My feet lead me to Ceres rock where I find a perch on those ancient stones. I open the bag and begin to spin, standing as I do so to let the spindle drop and rise, drop and rise, drop and rise. I am competent at spinning, but not talented. However, that night an eerie energy flattens out the knobbles, making my thread as smooth as Shadow's.

Whilst I spin, my thoughts drift. I find myself looking into two piercing grey eyes. Their intent expression makes me shiver as a sudden rush of warmth uncoils from beneath my belly. I have so many questions. Where did he get this sack of yarn? Who is he really? Why is he dressed as a peasant one time and a lord - a king? - the other? Why is he with his son? Who is his wife? Does he have more than one wife? Clearly, he travels a lot, and men like him always have a woman or two in every place they've passed through.

What would it be like to be his wife? whispers the voice in my head. My cheeks flame, becoming so hot that even my ears feel hot. I push that thought away. A man like that, full of arrogance and pride, would drop me like a hot stone from the oven once he'd had his way with me. Why would I even bother thinking about him? Men bring nothing but trouble.

My thoughts drift again. Why has Father locked us up? He imprisoned All-Gifted and me when we returned from that disastrous Bride Show in Constantinople. But our other sisters were already imprisoned. Clearly, something had happened while All-Gifted and I had been absent.

But what?

I always thought it had something to do with Protectress because she was so obviously power-hungry. I thought she had done something to enrage Father, which caused him to lock us up. But what about the snakes in her hair? Rumor said that she was being punished by the goddess Athena for doing something unthinkable in one of her temples. But Protectress always emphatically denied it, claiming she was being punished for something unthinkable that Death-Bringer had done.

I had always dismissed Protectress' claims, but then I couldn't stand her. No-one could. She was so cold, so calculating, so ruthless. And hadn't she recently proved all these qualities by murdering the one sister who competed with her for Father's favor? Her ruthless cleverness ensured that no one knew *she* was responsible. Even Father didn't know. But was I right to dismiss her claims? Supposing, for once, what she said was true, and it was Death-Bringer who was responsible for our imprisonment?

But what could Death-Bringer possibly have done? She always sat at her loom, spinning. She rarely went out. She had no friends, no companions, and certainly no lovers.

But had she always been like that?

I close my eyes, trying to remember what Death-Bringer had been like before All-Gifted and I left for the Bride Show. I see a smiling girl, holding a basket of flowers. I see a girl who was never still, who loved to skip out of the castle gates when we sisters trudged up those leafy slopes on early summer mornings to collect flowers and herbs that we would dry and distill into tonics and tinctures.

Death-Bringer had been so alive, so giddy, so giggling that others used to start when she was formally introduced.

"*Death-Bringer*?" they would gasp. "For a girl like that?" And so, they gave her a nickname. I search my memory. I believe they called her *Little Bee*. She stands before me, her reddish-gold hair bound up into braids that circle her head, decorated with green ribbons. Even in those, days, green was her favorite color, but it was not the wraith-like whitish-green that she favors now, but a darker shade that promised the hope of springtime.

What had happened to Death-Bringer? What had transformed her from that fun-loving fifteen-year-old to the grief-stricken older-than-twenty-five-year-old she is now?

I remember the many questions I asked. I remember how no one wanted to talk. But occasionally, people said things when they thought I wasn't around. At six, I was small for my age, and so I found a convenient nook in the depths of the kitchen where I would hide for hours on end, listening to Cook talk. I always hoped a traveler would visit, for not only would he bring news of the outside world, but Cook was usually more forthcoming, especially if he was handsome and liked to flirt. The only certain thing I could glean, however, was that Death-Bringer had been gathering flowers with our sisters one early summer morning when suddenly—she disappeared.

Poof!

Our sisters searched high and low for her, but they couldn't find her. I frown. I don't think I saw her again until one whole year had passed. By then, she was hunched in upon herself, sad and old-before-her-time, like she is now.

I was so shocked by her appearance; I could not believe she was my sister at first. She looked, not sixteen years old, but seventy-six years old, an ancient crone, bent, and beaten. Perhaps Father had beaten her, although he never said so. The night she arrived, under cover of darkness, Father called us together to tell us that Death-Bringer had been found in the forest, alone, disoriented, and seriously ill. It had taken months for her to recover, and when she did, he locked her in, just as he'd locked all of us up in that high tower.

But Father's bland explanation could not staunch the rumors. Travelers to the kitchen commented on how odd it was that Death-Bringer had been found a month after her disappearance by Father's men, and then taken away. They wondered why Father had punished her so severely. They speculated she must have taken a lover. Some even said she'd had a baby that had died.

I'd always dismissed this talk because who in the world would want Death-Bringer? She was so very unattractive. Then the image of her as that laughing fifteen-year-old girl appears in my mind's eye. Death-Bringer had been lovely, lovely enough to attract the notice of any passing male. Why hadn't I thought of that before?

Of course, she must have taken a lover. Of course, she must have had a baby. And that is why Father locked her up. That is why he continues to punish us all.

I return to my spinning. If I ever leave this accursed place, I would do so alone, without any man. My heart squeezes. Of course, I could not leave Shadow behind, my shy sister is so very vulnerable. And what about the littlest sisters, Bow, Sea-Foam, Ambiguity, and Treasure? I would take them with me too. Perhaps I could open a school for young women. Perhaps I could teach them something useful. Perhaps I could entice Maiden to come with me and teach them her medical skills.

A smile plays over my lips as the sun peeks over Ceres rock. I do not need a man to make me happy. I could make a happy life with my sisters.

FIFTEEN~

WELCOME TO THE BARDO

Justice continues her story

A month passes as I spin the yarn into thread, weave the thread into cloth and stitch the cloth with dark grey silk. I work in a trance trusting to something fierce within me. I have no plan, I just follow—something.

I begin my embroidery in the center doing flowers and leaves, but my hands add objects I would never have considered such as swords, daggers, ropes, wands. Then there are the water birds, bird-men, shallow-bottomed boats, oars. Lastly are the people, field-hands, oarsmen, aristocrats, princes.

As each one appears, I gaze at it. *Where has that come from?* Ropes, daggers and swords are everyday things to be found in a castle. Even wands revive memories of Morgana, and all the classes she taught us. But the other figures appear in a strange, unfamiliar style, standing sideways with limbs, faces and waists in profile, but with the shoulders and eyes to the front. Of course, I am familiar with field-hands, aristocrats and princes. But where have my representations of water-birds, oarsmen, shallow-bottom boats and oars come from? My sisters and I live in the mountains of Eastern Sikelia. We are not familiar with marshy lands or the people who inhabit them. Strangest of all are the bird-men with the head, shoulders and talons of a falcon, and the body of a man. The backs of my arms and my neck prickles. I feel as if I am in the hands of something very ancient. I shiver as the moon pours a waterfall of light onto my glimmering yarn.

Gradually as the embroidery takes shape, I realize a spiral thread of water runs through it, starting in the middle and coiling out to the edges of the cloth. By the time I put the last stitch of dark embroidery into the cloth, Shining has recovered from her sleeping sickness. Recovered, yes, I muse as I stitch the glimmering silver-grey cloth by the light of the waning moon, but not the same. She sits in our chamber with Death-Bringer, Shadow, and myself, quiet, dull-eyed, her sparkle gone.

On the first night of the dark moon, I wait until just after dusk until its faint crescent slides down below the trees. It is that time after supper when my sisters are readying for sleep. Silently, I walk into the center of our room and unfold the finished cloth. I hold it high above my head, like a silken scarf, and then let go. As the cloth floats, a puff of dust (or is it smoke) rises up obscuring everything. The cloth spreads itself out, my embroidery shining darkly in the gloom. Slowly, oh-so-slowly it lands on the floor.

As it slides to a halt, my embroidery blazes silver-white for an instant, then there is a grating sound like an iron door on a rusty hinge, as the floor turns, opening up a spiral that exactly matches the spiral I have just finished. The grating grows louder as the floor unfolds like a flower, like a moonflower rotating towards the rising moon. After several moments the noise ceases, the dust settles, revealing a spiral of steps leading below.

The steps look as if they have just been completed by Father's masons. The wall of the stair shaft is smooth, lit at intervals by torches. The stairs are shallow, enticing, easy for even a tumbling toddler to try, suitable for women wearing dainty slippers. The stairs wind down—where?

Before I can utter any word of warning Death-Bringer pushes forward. "Come sisters," she says, her face unusually bright. "What are you waiting for? We are free!"

The littlest ones run after her laughing, while I exchange looks with my left-behind sisters. All-Gifted looks thoughtful. Shining and Maiden smile. Even Shadow looks hopeful.

"What kind of trick is this?" snaps Protectress turning on me.

But before I have time to reply, screams whirl up from below.

We hurry down those steps, launching ourselves so precipitously we don't notice the spiral door clicking shut above us. We don't notice the stairs steepening, the walls roughening, or the air growing colder, exuding a dank sulfurous odor. By the time we reach Treasure, the torches have sputtered out and it is dark, as dark as a nightmare.

As my eyes gradually adjust to the murk, I notice writhing shapes detaching themselves from the wall, dropping to the ground where they curl around my sisters' ankles, paralyzing them with shock. Other creatures emerge, but it is too dark to see.

"Welcome to the Bardo," scrapes a voice. "The home of the in-between. Whither do you wish to go?"

"We wish for freedom," I say, speaking in the direction of the voice. I fold my arms to hide my trembling fingers. It is so dark I cannot see the creature.

"We have been locked up by our tyrannical father," says Death-Bringer, her voice the color of silver, the silver thread of water that runs through my embroidery. "It is time, well past time," she continues, "for us to be free. While we languish in our father's tower, the outside passes us by, like an inexorably flowing stream. We grow older by the day, yet nothing happens. 'Tis a living death."

The creature makes a gasping sound, which could pass for a laugh. "And so," it scrapes out, "you wish to escape death."

"We are young women," I reply. "Some of us are very young."

"And some of you are not so young. Your eldest has thirty autumns. Many of her age have already passed on—through this doorway."

I ball my hands into fists to stop them from shaking, trying to calm my spiraling thoughts.

"I have been dead all my life long," retorts All-Gifted. She emerges from the shadows, a faint glow emanating from her, making her look taller than usual. Gone is the usual bent shape that causes men's eyes to flick over her towards the younger princesses. Now, she stands straight and magnificent.

"I have a right to my own life," she growls. "If you won't help, then I will lead my sisters to freedom!"

The being cackles. "Good luck to your ladyship." I see a movement as if someone or something is bowing. "May the goddess grant you a long and prosperous death." It cackles again. "Don't say I didn't warn you."

It stands aside, its dark robes swirling. "Please." It makes a gesture with its arm. "Don't let me stop you."

My whole body shakes as my scalp prickles with ice. I look back the way we've come, but the stairs, the lights, even the walls have vanished. We float in a haze of indeterminacy.

The creature comes towards me, placing a scaly paw on my arm. I freeze, unable to move. "If you encounter trouble," it hisses, "look for the Polaris star. Close by, you will see *The Snake of the Sky*. Follow along its entire length and you will reach Polaris, the Pole Star."

"The snake in the sky?" I look up at the stars that are suddenly blazing above us. "What snake?"

The creature clicks its tongue impatiently. "It goes by many names. Some call it *The Haymaker's Way*. Some call it *The Bird's Path*. Some call it *The Winter Street, The Fire Stream, The River of Light*, or even *Heaven's River*. Then there are some who persist in calling it *The Milky Way,* although a more stupid name, I can't imagine. Whatever you call it, it is a scarf of light, of indigos, blues, purples, and pinks. Follow that path to Polaris."

"But why?"

"It is *The Way of the Dead,*" it replies. "It is where dead souls go. After death, you understand."

I nod as if I understand, and the creature makes a gurgling sound in its throat. "You don't understand, do you?" It gives me a pat. "You. Save your sisters."

"Why me?"

"You are the seventh daughter, the one bearing power and luck. Go meet your destiny."

It vanishes in a skirl of dead leaves. We stand there, back in the swirl of darkness, thrust into a stretching silence of coldness and death. Even the snakes have slithered away.

I take the hands of the two youngest, Ambiguity and Treasure, and move forward. A slight sound by my feet makes me stop. Water bubbles up, sliding smoothly downhill. I follow the sound, step by step.

By the river, there's a grove of trees, sings Treasure

In the grove, there stood an empty boat, continues Ambiguity

By the boat there stood a princely figure, they both end laughing

Apple, Apple, fallen in the water, sings Ambiguity

By the stream, I took the prince's hand, continues Treasure

And he rowed me all the way across, they both end laughing

The trickle becomes a runnel, the runnel becomes a stream, the stream becomes a torrent ending in a roaring waterfall. Edging along with the children, I see faint splashes of color. Looking up, I see we are indeed in a grove of trees. But these are jewel trees, trees growing rubies, trees with lapis lazuli flowers, trees that dangle gigantic coral clusters like dates. Everywhere, enormous jewels sparkle from their branches: emerald, sapphire, diamond, pearl.

I look up and marvel at it all. Where are we? Is this Paradise? Is this the garden of the gods and goddesses? Or is it the Garden of Eden? I bite my lip as the jewel trees dazzle, their light showing the raging waterfall ending in a deep pool, as peaceful and quiet as death.

Next to the shore stand twelve boats. Next to each boat stands a princely figure. Each figure bows, as mesmerized, we allow ourselves to be helped in and rowed to the other side.

Silence envelops us. Even the oars make no sound as they slip in and out of the water. On the other side is darkness.

Nothing.

SIXTEEN

GILGAMESH

Justice continues her story

At length, something happens, a stir, a subtle shift of color. A figure looms up, a giant of a man, almost as broad as he is tall.

"I am The-Ancestor-Is-Hero!" he bellows, "Surpassing-All-Other-Kings. Look at my body, ye mighty, and despair. No one can best me in Wrestling—"

A gust of papery laughter grazes my ear. The creature in the dark robes reappears. "Gilgamesh!" it calls, "For such is your name. No one has come to wrestle with Gilgamesh, the King of Uruk. For you are not here to wrestle, my lord, but to find your friend

Enkidu, the wild man. You want the gift of immortality so that you can bring Enkidu back from the world of the dead. For that, you must perform a task."

"MUST?" bellows Gilgamesh. "I am the King of Kings. I have looked into the deep, the abyss, the unknown. You cannot tell *me* what to do!"

The creature folds its arms and laughs again. "Do you know who I am? I am KEH-ruhn, Charon, the gatekeeper of the underworld. I row the souls across the dead river. I decide who comes and who goes. If you cannot pay me my fee, *you* will wander by the shores of the river that divides the living from the dead for one thousand years." It leans forward. "Do you wish to see Enkidu or not?"

Gilgamesh drops to his knees, tearing his hair, bellowing his grief. The sounds of sorrow deafen, the dying throes of a wounded beast. Eventually, Gilgamesh quietens, soft gulping sobs erupting from his throat.

"If you wish to see Enkidu," remarks Charon, "you will do as I say."

Slowly, Gilgamesh nods his head.

"You will go to this tunnel, which no man has ever entered." He gestures with his hand and our tunnel appears, with its smooth walls and flickering torches. Two scorpions appear at its mouth. "First, you must persuade the scorpions to let you enter." Charon steps back, his dark robes swirling. "Please." He bows low.

The scorpions are not the small scuttling creatures I know. Instead, they are half-dragon, half-man. They are magnificent, huge, fire-breathing, terrifying. They glow as golden as the sun. I cover my eyes, just peeking through my fingers.

All-Gifted appears. "I bear the sigil of Scorpio," she remarks. "I can help you, my lord Gilgamesh. If you wish."

At his nod, she flicks her fingers, the light of the dragon men dimming. "Do not look directly at them," All-Gifted remarks. "Their stare strikes death into men."

Slowly, as if in a daze, the giant Gilgamesh lumbers towards them, his eyes averted.

The larger dragon-man opens its mouth. "Why have you come on so great a journey?"

"Where am I?" Gilgamesh studies the ground.

"You are in Mashu," says the smaller dragon-man. "The great cedar mountain in the roots of an ancient cedar tree. The world tree. The sacred tree. The only tree to survive the great destruction. Mashu guards the rising and setting sun."

"For what have you traveled so far?" asks the larger dragon-man.

"For Enkidu," replies Gilgamesh. "I loved him profoundly. Together we endured calamity, catastrophe, disaster. I come for him. I wept for him day and night. I refused his body for burial. I thought my friend would come back because of my weeping. Since he went, life is nothing."

There is a long silence as the dragon-men glare at Gilgamesh. "Tell me the real reason for your coming," says the larger one.

Gilgamesh sighs. "I have come to find everlasting life. I am here to question my grandfather Noah, concerning the living and the dead. Noah, who survived the great flood. Noah who saved the animals by following the word of God above. Noah who entered the assembly of the gods and found everlasting life."

"No man has done what you have asked," hisses the larger dragon-man. "No man has gone into the roots of the world tree. How stupid can you be? The length of it is twelve leagues of darkness. There is no light. Your soul will be awed, frozen, petrified by darkness. From the setting sun to the rising sun there is no light."

Gilgamesh glances at the dragon-men and immediately lowers his head. "Although I should go in sorrow and in pain, with sighing and with weeping, still, I must go. Open the gate to the underneath of the world tree."

The smaller dragon-man shifts his lips into something that suggests a smile. "Go, Gilgamesh. I permit you to pass through the mountain of Mashu, the underneath of the world tree. May your feet carry you safely home. The gate of the mountain is open."

SEVENTEEN

THE LABORS OF GILGAMESH

Justice continues her story

Charon steps forward, his dark robes swirling. "Before you enter, hear me." He holds up his hand. "You must outrun the sun for twelve hours, between sunset and sunrise. To ensure your compliance, I will time each hour. Each princess will stand guard for one hour, with her consort."

He turns, his robes swirling. "For hour one, we have Lady Death-Bringer now Queen Puh-SEFF-oh-nee with her husband Prince Unseen, now King HAY-dees of the Underworld."

Before he can motion them forward, I put my hand on his scaly arm. "Where did you get those names? I whisper. *Death-Bringer* is her name, not *Persephone*."

He rounds on me, his bluish-grey eyes flashing. "*Persephone* is what we call *Death-Bringer* in Greek. Do you not understand this?"

I shake my head. Yes, we speak Greek in Sikelia, for that is the language or the merchants. But the names we give each other belong to that curious admixture of other languages that have floated to our shores over the vastness or time. Is everything to be Greek now? Are the culture and ancient traditions of Sikelia to be set aside for the benefit of Greek colonists who keep appearing on our shores, unwanted and un-welcomed?

"*Death-Bringer* is a translation of *Persephone,*" hisses Charon. "From *pherein phonon,* to bring or cause death. Just as *Unseen* is a translation of *Hades*." He flicks his wrist and Death-Bringer *Persephone* appears. She is fifteen again, her reddish-gold hair bound up into braids that circle her head, decorated with green ribbons. With her is a shadowy figure, in robes of green that are so dark, they look almost black. He bends over her, his silvery eyes unable to look away from her hopeful loveliness. A dullish glow emanating from his forehead indicates a crown. Slowly, he places a golden circlet on her braids. Persephone looks up at her husband, laughing, bestowing a kiss on his cheek.

And then I notice the baby she holds.

"Princess Quince," murmurs Charon into my ear. I jump and turn. He'd moved so silently I hadn't noticed him. "Meh-lih-NOH-ee," he murmurs again, "in our Greek Language. The baby who caused all the trouble."

I nod, remembering our long, long, long years in the tower. That life now seems so very far away.

Persephone holds baby Melinoë high in the air so that I can see her properly for the very first time. She has yellow skin, green eyes the shape of almonds, and black hair that runs like a waterfall down her back.

Suddenly, Ambiguity appears out of the gloom that hovers near the lake, bearing torches that she uses to light the entrance of our tunnel. Then she drifts towards a stone tower, moving up a spiral staircase until it is lit within. She is followed by Persephone, who takes her place on the roof with her husband and daughter.

"Queen Persephone, King Hades, and their baby daughter Princess Melinoë will act as watchers for the first hour," intones Charon.

As Gilgamesh enters our tunnel, following the path of the invisible sun during nighttime hours, the torches flick off. By the time Gilgamesh completes the first hour, the darkness becomes as black as a bottomless well. All light has been extinguished. He can see nothing. My third sister Queen Persephone, her husband the King of the Underworld, and their child Princess Melinoë descend the stairs and vanish.

"Lady Intrigue, now Princess Kly-tuhm-NESS-truh of Sparta will watch for hour two, with her new husband, yours truly, Lord Charon." Charon scrapes out.

I turn to stare at him. How has he managed to persuade Intrigue to marry him? He is so very unattractive.

Intrigue appears, scowling. "My name is *Intrigue,*" she spits out.

Lord Charon curves his lips upwards into a smile. At least, it would be a smile if it reached his eyes, and if it did not show a mouthful of broken and cracked teeth in various stages of decay. I study him. His smile is really a grimace, as if he were in pain.

"Come, my love," he purrs, or attempts to purr in his raspy voice. He puts a scaly hand on her arm.

Intrigue flinches and draws away.

"I explained your name to you," he continues in his purr-rasp. "Clytemnestra means *celebrated plotter,* from *klutós* meaning *celebrated* and *medomai,* to *plan or be cunning*. It is your name in Greek."

"I am *not* a celebrated plotter!" Intrigue stamps her foot.

Charon throws back his head, gurgling with raspy laughter that ends in a cough. "My dear," he remarks, wiping his eyes, "what got you into this difficulty in the first place? You were conniving to take Protectress's place as lady of the land were you not? Unfortunately for you, she proved to be even more cunning.

Which is why you are in the underworld. With me." He bestows his grimace of a smile on Intrigue, who shudders and backs away.

"I am dead!" she wails. "I will never again see the sun set or the moon rise. Never hear the hoot of the midnight owl. Never see the hare scamper through the damp grasses of dawn, or the morning mists coiling off the lake. Never feel the susurrating wind on my cheeks or hear the soothing soughing of the sea." She turns to us. "I am dead, my sisters. Whereas all of you are alive." She dissolves into gulping sobs, like a baby crying.

Charon sighs, holding her awkwardly against his scaly chest. "You are quite wrong, my love," he soothes. "We are all dead here."

Intrigue raises her tear-stained face.

"I am dead," explains Charon patiently. "And have been for some time. You died last month. Your sister, Queen Persephone died ten years ago."

"But—" I stare at him. "But she was with us in the tower."

"Not really," says Charon. "The light in her eyes went out when she lost her baby and husband. She endured ten years as punishment for what she did. For finding her lover-husband. For having a love-child. For ruining all of your reputations, and your marriage prospects."

Tears well in my eyes. "I had no idea. I was never angry with her."

"That is because you did not know," replies Charon. "And now she is free. She is happy with her husband and baby. She is the Queen of the Underworld. Dead. Residing here below."

I wipe my eyes. "We will never see her again."

"Not unless you die," he replies.

"This is not fair!" exclaims Intrigue. "I may be dead, but you, my sisters are cursed! Shining will start a war."

How does she know that? I ask myself. Has death given her the power of seeing into the future?

"Shadow and Treasure will be war prizes," continues Intrigue, "slaves to the men who—"

"And you," I interrupt. "What will happen to you?"

"I'm already dead," snaps Intrigue *Clytemnestra,* "so what does it matter?"

"You will have an interesting welcome waiting for your husband after the war is over," remarks Ambiguity.

Of course, Ambiguity is a seer. It is one of her special powers, one she has been perfecting with that silver bowl brimful of water that she keeps next to her bed.

"You will create a great deal of mischief," continues Ambiguity, "with your cunning weaving—"

"Ladies, Ladies!" interposes Charon. "It is cruel to keep Gilgamesh waiting any longer. He must run his second hour." He proffers his arm to Intrigue and bows low. "Come, my love, we must watch." They mount the lighted spiral stairs to the castle roof, standing tall and magnificent.

By the time Gilgamesh completes the first two hours, any fresh breezes have ceased. Endless darkness stretches before him. My eighth sister, Princess Clytemnestra of Sparta, descends the stairs and vanishes. Her new husband, Lord Charon, gatekeeper to the underworld, remains.

"Lady Shining, now Princess Helen of Sparta," intones Charon, "with Lord Playful, son of Nobody, will watch for the third hour." Shining, her old sparkle back, clothed in one of her translucent dresses, bats her eyes at Playful who turns a vibrant red and averts his eyes.

After three hours, any fresh air has gone. The weight of darkness presses in upon Gilgamesh. My fourth sister Princess Helen of Sparta and Prince Playful (her new plaything) descend the tower and vanish.

"Lady Shadow, now Princess Brih-say-iss," intones Charon, "with Lord Darkness, son of Chaos, Lord of Reality, will watch for the fourth hour."

My sixth sister Princess Briseis glides into place with Erebus, Prince of Darkness. After four hours, the darkness thickens, becoming as stale as the inside of a felted tent. There is no light. Gilgamesh can see nothing ahead and nothing behind.

"Lady Maiden, now Princess Koh-ray," intones Charon, "with her unicorn companion, will keep watch for the fifth hour."

My fifth sister Princess Kore appears, her arms around the neck of a unicorn. After five hours, the air burns like the inside of an oven.

There is no light. It is as black as pitch. Gilgamesh can see nothing ahead and nothing behind him.

My tenth sister Sea-Foam, now the goddess Aphrodite, keeps watch for the sixth hour with Ares, Lord War. After six hours, the murky air turns as suffocating as a sandstorm, every step causing Gilgamesh to wheeze heavily.

My ninth sister Bow, now the goddess Artemis keeps watch for the seventh hour with Apollo, Lord Oracle. After seven hours, the darkness solidifies, stopping Gilgamesh's ears, mouth, and eyes.

My eldest sister All-Gifted, now Princess Pandora, keeps watch for the eighth hour with her companion, the goddess Athena. When he has gone eight hours Gilgamesh gives a muffled scream, for the darkness heats, as if he is wading through a vat of scalding honey.

My second sister Protectress, now Princess Medusa, keeps watch for the ninth hour with Poseidon, Lord Sea. After nine hours, Gilgamesh senses a breath of wind on his face. He coughs up great clumps of mud. His breathing eases. But the darkness continues thick and murky.

My eleventh sister Ambiguity, now the goddess Hecate, keeps watch for the tenth hour with Osiris, Lord Afterlife. After ten hours the end is near. Gilgamesh draws in lungfuls of crisp air.

"Lady Treasure, now Princess Chris-say-iss of Troy," intones Charon, "with Lord Deity, will keep watch for the eleventh hour." My youngest sister Princess Chryseis appears, her hand on arm of Zeus, Lord Deity. After eleven hours the disk of the sun appears above the horizon.

"Lastly, Lady Justice, now Princess Callidice, with her admirer Lord Nobody, will keep watch for the twelfth hour," remarks Charon.

I start. So involved am I in this strange procession of my sisters with their new identities and companions I'd not noticed that Charon had yet to call my name. Now I am to be paired with *Nobody*. What does that mean? Are we married? Are we engaged? Am I fated to marry him? But he appears, bowing low with a flourish, and so I ascend the spiral stairs with him.

At the end of twelve hours the sun lifts into the sky onto a beautiful Autumnal day. Gilgamesh gives a great cry as he raises his arms in the air. "Enkidu, I come!" he shouts, before becoming one with the rising sun.

EIGHTEEN~

THE VASTNESS OF ABSENCE

Justice continues her story

Lord Nobody takes my hand and kisses it with a courtly flourish. He straightens and probes me with his steely grey eyes. Except that his eyes are not steely but soft, as soft as those clouds that produce soft spring showers to kiss my cheek.

Slowly, oh-so-slowly, he angles his head until I feel the pressure of his lips upon mine. His lips are soft and warm, gentle and respectful.

"Princess Callidice," he murmurs.

He deepens his kiss, a man thirsty for something. My cheeks burn as I realize that I am melting into him, my body finding the perfect curve as I nestle again him. My heart beats out a rapid fusillade. I grit my teeth and yank myself away.

He blinks in surprise.

I stare up at him. "Don't tell me," I remark. "*Callidice* is a translation of *Justice*."

"*Beautiful* Justice," he murmurs, winding his fingers through my hair, as his lips find mine again.

Strange sensations uncoil beneath my belly, making me feel warm and sluggish as if I'd just awoken from a beguiling dream. With the greatest effort, I disengage myself from him and move away, lifting my chin to glare.

He grins and takes a step towards me. "You've never felt the touch of a man before." It is a statement, not a question.

I grind my jaw and shake my head. "You presume too much." My voice is cool. "Take me home."

"Back to your tower-prison? To the accursed tomb?" He leans closer, his lips full, pink, moist. "Is that really what you want?"

I tear my eyes away from his probing grey ones, step back, and nod my head.

And just like that, I am lying in bed, back in my chamber. The sun is rising as I roll out of bed. Quietly, I tiptoe around the room, checking on my sisters. They are all there, slumbering peacefully. The floor is back in its place. Everything is in order.

I open the casement above my bed and lean out. Father's workers are already in the fields harvesting. A cool breeze laps my cheeks as a nightingale trills an arpeggio. It is as if nothing has happened.

But I cannot forget his kiss. My cheeks warm. Why had I allowed him to come so close? I let out an enormous sigh as I continue to gaze out the window. What is wrong with me? My brow furrows as my jaw ticks. I will pay for this later with one of my debilitating headaches. But right now, I am furious. I am beyond furious—with him.

I am old enough to know the costs of consorting with a man. I don't want intimacy. I don't want to be in his arms. I shudder as I imagine how it would be, our naked bodies touching one another, his on top of me, his grey eyes gazing at mine as he joins us together—.

I huff out an exasperated breath, then catch myself. The last thing I want now is for my sisters to awaken.

I don't want lovemaking, because I don't want to die young trying to push his child out or me. Plus, I know all too well how easily distracted men are. Look at Father. He has another concubine every day. They may gaze at you with soft grey eyes. They may seem to probe into your soul. They may get down on their knees, one hand pressed to their heart and make the most spectacular of promises. But nothing lasts. They will be gone before you know it.

Nobody is just like other men. He will treat me as badly as All-Gifted was treated at the Bride Show. He doesn't really care for me; he just wants to possess my body. He doesn't admire me. He doesn't love me. I will just be another conquest, another notch on his tally stick. Besides where is his wife?

A light breeze slips in, as the voice in my head whispers *You know that what you say is not true. You like him very much indeed. He is perfect for you. He is brilliant, cunning, perceptive. And he loves you. You should marry him.*

I drop down onto my bed, and pace around the room. I check the other beds again for my sisters, and it is only then that I realize that both Intrigue's and Death-Bringer's beds are now empty. How come I didn't see that before? I glance up, out of the window. The sun is now high in the sky. It must have been a trick of the light.

Although two of my sisters are now gone, it is Death-Bringer's death that clutches at my heart. Perhaps I saw what I expected to see or wanted to see. I thought I saw her slumbering beneath her bedsheet. But she is gone. Gone forever. I shall not see her again until Death takes me.

The breeze sighs again, as I shiver, taking in the vastness of absence.

NINETEEN~

THE RUINED SLIPPERS

Justice continues her story

Days pass as I sink back into being a prisoner in Father's tower, along with my nine surviving sisters. Why, oh why did I refuse Nobody's request to stay with him and leave my prison forever?

I ask myself this question several times a day, looking up from my scissors as I alter the left-behind robes of my absent sisters to fit the ones who survive. My sisters tell me I am the best seamstress of all. When I am in a sunny mood, I try to believe them. When in a sour mood, as I am today, I know it is because not a one of them has the patience to make these alterations.

I sigh as I put my hand to my head, trying to knead away the inevitable headache. *You do not trust him*, remarks the voice in my head.

So, what would have happened if I'd accepted his request? It is not hard to imagine. I would be spending hours in his bed. I shudder as I shove that thought away. I would probably be breeding now, carrying his child. Which means that my life would now be measured out in months, not years, and I could look forward to an agonizing, excruciating death.

I push that thought away too as I rise up onto my stool to open the window, letting in the soft breaths of an autumnal evening. I linger for a while before turning to back to the unnaturally silent room. My sisters sit at their various tasks. Silent.

Something essential has gone from us since Death-Bringer's disappearance, or rather, her death. Death-Bringer - *or rather Persephone - I correct myself*, for with the arrival of Nobody, we have a multitude of men speaking Greek with his pure accent. And so, Father decreed that we change our names from Sikelian to Greek.

"Why?" Ambiguity *Hecate* asks one day.

"Perhaps Father finally means to marry us off," mutters Protectress *Medusa.*

It is understandable that the death of Intrigue *Clytemnestra* would cause a deafening silence. No longer does she stride into the room, clad in her latest finery, twirling for the littlest ones and even - if she were in a good mood - allowing them to borrow her bracelets and necklaces. Her death causes the littlest ones to wilt into an unnatural silence, whilst Persephone's absence makes them restless.

And so Shining *Helen* fills the void left by Intrigue *Clytemnestra*. Of all of us, Helen is the most like Clytemnestra with her laughter, her head tosses, and the endless hours she spends washing her hair, taking baths and applying makeup. Now that Clytemnestra is no longer around, Helen absconds with her entire wardrobe, asking me to alter the clothes that her tinier sister had worn to fit her taller, more voluptuous form. I am so busy cutting open Clytemnestra's magnificent dresses, making them into tunics that can be worn over Helen's translucent robes, that I fail to notice our littlest sisters.

Until the night when I find I cannot sleep.

It is the fifth hour, the time when Maiden *Kore* kept watch as Gilgamesh stumbled through the tunnel into air that was as hot as an oven. It is still. Nothing twists the living leaves of the trees or lifts the dead leaves from the hard-packed earth. Not a bird sings, they are all asleep, their heads tucked into their wings. So how do my sisters disappear so silently?

Something about our room seems strange. I lift myself up on my left elbow and peer through the murky darkness. Something is wrong. Quietly, I roll out of bed and tiptoe around the room. All-Gifted *Pandora,* Protectress *Medusa* and Maiden *Kore* are breathing peacefully in their beds. But where is Shining *Helen*? Shadow *Briseis*? Where are the littlest ones, Bow *Artemis,* Sea-Foam *Aphrodite,* Ambiguity *Hecate,* and Treasure *Chryseis*?

Slowly, I move into the center of the room and see a corner of my embroidered cloth peeking out in the middle of the room.

I freeze. What should I do? I find myself walking, as if in a trance, to that magical spiral, as the floor turns like the dark-flowered belladonna raising its head to the moon. Slowly I descend a step, and then another. After seven steps, my head is just beneath the floor. Something pulls me up short.

I cannot do it. I cannot go down into that dark tunnel with its spiders, bats, snakes, and other slithering beings. I cannot meet the icy eyes of Lord Charon. I cannot go through the magical grove to the enchanted lake, get into a spell-bound boat and ride across to that cursed castle. What if I never get back? What if I find myself in yet another trap, cursed to remain there for a thousand years or more? What if going down those steps means that I am creating my own death?

Hastily, I turn and rush back up those steps, tripping over my robes in my haste to do so. There is a groaning noise of iron upon iron as the floor turns and the door in the floor snaps shut. I roll up onto my knees, before realizing that it has a good chunk of my bed-robe in its maw. I wriggle out of my clothing and stare in dismay at my ruined garment, before shivering violently. Quickly, I hurry to

Clytemnestra's clothes-keep, finding one of her fur wraps to envelop me.

I spend the next five hours, seated on my stool, waiting. As the sun rises above Ceres' rock, my seven sisters troop in, before flinging themselves onto their beds and sinking into a too-deep sleep.

Quietly, I move among them, taking their slippers of their feet before tucking them in.

Every one of their slippers is ruined, as if they have been dancing in a frenzy all night long.

I sit, frozen for an hour or so. What can I do? There is only one person who can help.

In the end, I laboriously inscribe a message for Nobody, telling him I wish to meet him in the garden after supper. I descend onto the bedewed lawn of the garden and put this message into the hands of a young boy working in the gardens.

"Go to the stables," I tell him, putting a silver piece into his hand. "And give this to Nobody. Make sure that no-one sees you."

The boy's eyes widen as he gazes at the coin. Then he secretes the coin and letter away, before nodding his head and running off.

I sigh. Now I must think of the best way of approaching him. Should I use my womanly wiles like Clytemnestra or Helen? Or should I be more like Kore?

My pride decides that I must keep my dignity. I pray to the goddess Athena that squashing my raging thoughts will allow me to treat my admirer with the coolness he deserves.

TWENTY~

Twelve Dancing Princesses

Justice continues her story

He appears at dusk, this time looking like a peasant in sun-beaten clothes, his feet grimy, his head covered in a disintegrating straw hat. I do not need to treat him as a stranger for he puts on a brilliant performance as an over-awed serf, not sure why milady would want to speak with the likes of him.

I sigh. How can I possibly have a serious conversation when he behaves like that?

At that exact moment, he beckons with a soil-encrusted hand, and we slide into the shade of a massive tree. All pretense gone, he takes my hand and brushes his lips over it, ending with a kiss in my palm, before folding my fingers over it.

I arch my brow. Of course, I am used to courtly ways and the silly displays men put on to impress the ladies. But there is no one else but me. I stare at him long and hard, stifling my many questions about him, his family, his son, and whether he currently has a wife.

"She is dead," he remarks at length.

I start, my cheeks heating like a cauldron on the boil. "Your—your wife?"

He throws back his head and gives a great belly of a laugh, stopping suddenly as he catches the expression on my face. "I was talking of Persephone, the sister you miss the most."

"Oh." I hang my head, suffused with embarrassment, cursing myself for the way in which I'd let him trip me up so easily. And how did he know that it was Death-Bringer I missed so much?

"You asked me to come," he says gently, "because you are worried about your sisters."

My mind clears. "It has been a week since it began. Night after night, I wake to the eerie silence of our room. Pandora and Medusa sleep as if enchanted by a powerful potion, while my seven other sisters disappear as darkness coils around the room, not reappearing until the first rays of the sun side across the wooden floor. My sisters are exhausted, dark circles ringing their eyes as they tumble into their beds without undressing or even taking their slippers off."

He takes my hand, his grey eyes pinned on mine.

"What do I *do*?" I exclaim to Nobody.

"Ask yourself why three of your sisters are sleeping like the dead, while your other sisters flee the tower to dance."

I frown. "They must have drunk a sleeping potion. But how?"

"That is for you to find out," he squeezes my hand. "And if that is so, why is it that you are the only one to notice?"

I gaze up into his well-lined face. "I don't know."

"Find out," he whispers before vanishing into the gloaming.

I stare after him, for the first time feeling lost. I realize suddenly how much I value his judgement. He knows so much and always asks the most relevant questions. If we were to form a partnership, I think as the evening breeze lifts my veil, we would be formidable indeed. Thoughtfully, I return to the tower.

Gradually, my sisters begin to dance all day long. They would reappear at dawn, fling themselves onto their beds, then awaken and start dancing. I try to stop them, but their eyes are glassy and unseeing. One by one, they arise from their beds, swirl down the stone stairs that lead from our chamber to the gardens outside, where they would circle the tower a few times before whirling their way into the village. The folk take to calling them the *Twelve Dancing Princesses,* even though only half of us participate.

Reluctantly, I go to Father. "You must stop this!" I exclaim. You cannot want your unmarried daughters to make a spectacle of themselves in public. You cannot want them to be the butt of rude jokes, of endless speculation about their reputations."

But Father seems not to hear. He stares at me absently, without seeing, then returns to his desk covered over by scrolls.

Again, I summon Nobody. "What is going on?" I ask him. "Father never sits by his desk all day. He is always out and about on horseback."

Nobody coughs. "Some say your father cannot provide dowries for all his daughters. That his money has run dry—"

I wheel away from him, embarrassed that he knows so much about our family affairs when I know nothing. I run upstairs to our chamber and find Medusa fanning herself on her bed.

"Is this true?" I gasp, running up the final stairs and collapsing onto the floor beside her bed.

She wrinkles her nose as she takes me in, and indeed I must look a sight, with my hair wild and my clothes disarranged by running. "Where have you been? You look like a hoyden. What is Father going to say when he sees you?"

"But that's just the point," I shout. "Father doesn't care about anything. He doesn't care that all of our sisters are dancing madly around the village, followed by laughing men who sing bawdy songs and crack crude jokes. He seems to care nothing for our reputations."

She sits up. "How do you know that?"

"I've just been to see him, and when I told him all this, he just sat there staring at his scrolls."

"What does Lord Nobody say?"

I flush. Unfortunately, all my sisters are all-too-aware that Nobody is my admirer. I take a deep breath. "He told me that Father cannot provide dowries for all of us. That his money has run dry—"

"Did he, indeed?" She rises to her feet. "That cheap bastard," she mutters. "No wonder he has locked us up these ten years."

"Medusa!" I exclaim. "You cannot talk about Father like that!"

"Can't I?" she folds her arms and glares. "Not even when he has ruined our lives? I will see him myself!" And she stomps off before I can stop her.

TWENTY-ONE

The Death of Shadow

Justice continues her story

As the days cool, as the evenings draw in, Shadow *Briseis* fades. Unable to rise from her bed one morning, she is left behind as her sisters fly down the stairs for their now daily dance through the village. I, however, spend hours, days sitting with her.

"You should not be here." Her voice is a wisp. "You should be outside enjoying what little freedom Father allows you."

"But I am happy to sit here with you." I squeeze her hand.

She tries to squeeze my hand back, but her touch is too weak.

I brush her dark hair away from her face, my stomach tightening as I take in how grey her face has become. It is almost as if my shadow of a sister is dissolving before my eyes.

"I have to go," she murmurs.

"But how will I exist without you?"

A faint smile turns the corners of her lips up. "You have your man, your Nobody. Do you not see? He loves you. He will do anything for you." She turns her head to the wall.

A pitter-patter of feet sounds as my sisters return to our tower. Suddenly, a cry goes up, and I hear my sisters behind me wailing. Reluctantly, I turn. Ambiguity *Hecate* has fallen into a faint. I hurry over, a mirror in my hand. She is still breathing but cannot be roused from her death-like sleep.

After that, the littlest ones succumb like saplings felled by a storm when the large oak has gone. One by one, Bow *Artemis*, Sea-Foam *Aphrodite*, and Treasure *Chryseis* follow their sisters and half-sisters.

"Someone must tell Father," I say.

Protectress *Medusa* glares. "What's holding *you* back?"

"I am the seventh daughter. Surely you, or Shining *Helen* or All-Gifted *Pandora* should do it."

Medusa folds her arms. "I'm not so foolish as to bring such bad news to Father again."

Father had been enraged when she'd confronted him about his lack of money, threatening to throw her out and feed her to the wolves if she ever dared question his authority again.

She turns to Helen. "What about you, Shining Light?"

But Helen is slumped on her bed, her eyes dull. I peer at her. Is she about to fall ill too?

"I shall go to Father," I say.

Medusa gives a cold laugh. "Much good that will do you."

I ignore her. "Who will come with me?"

Pandora and Maiden *Kore* raise their heads.

We put on our finest robes to attract Father's eye, I insisting he would take us more seriously if we presented ourselves as the princesses we were. Then, escorted by Father's guards, we make our way from the tower to his throne room.

Father keeps us waiting outside for some time.

Tears blur Pandora's face. "There is nothing I can do to save our sisters. Father never listens to me."

I touch her arm. "Hush now. Father doesn't like tears." I draw a thin triangle of silk out of my sleeve and give it to her. "Our plan is to persuade Father to let us out of his tower. We should ask him to send us to the summer palace that lies along the shore of Saragusa."

"But he would never send us there!" exclaims Kore. "It is rife with pirate ships. We could be kidnapped."

"I'm suggesting it as our opening gambit. You should always ask first for what you do not think you will get," I reply, repeating some advice Nobody had given me.

"But not if it means that you're going to insult your opponent. Father will just shut down if you suggest such a thing and fly off into one of his rages!"

"What do *you* suggest then?"

Kore is silent for a long moment. Eventually, Pandora moves forward, her face now free of tears. "What about the nunnery of St Katharine? It is only a mile away and we could legitimately tell Father that his daughters need the expert treatment of the good sisters."

I gape at her. "I didn't know you were such a Christian."

She hands back my silken handkerchief. "I am not, but I think this ploy is likely to find favor with Father. We can agree to let Father post his guards around the nunnery."

"But how will that achieve anything?" asks Kore. "We will never get out then."

Pandora glances at me. "There are ways and means," she says smiling faintly. "And don't forget the littlest ones have powers of their own."

I stare at her. Pandora, with her strange ways, her constant mutterings and murmurings over her evil-smelling cauldron seems so out of it, that it hadn't occurred to me that she'd noticed that at least three of our youngest have goddess powers.

Eventually, the doors open and we are led inside to see Father. Pandora presents our case to him tactfully, but cogently. But Father is strangely apathetic, sitting and staring at nothing, almost as if he is in a trance.

At length Pandora puts her finger to her lips, and we leave.

"We should leave as soon as possible," remarks Kore.

"This evening," I say.

But when we return to our round chamber, all thoughts of leaving flee our minds. For Shadow *Briseis* has passed beyond the veil.

I kneel down beside her bed, holding her cold hand in mine, my eyes hazy with tears, my body shaking uncontrollably with sobs. What has happened? Nothing has bitten Briseis, no-one has tried to throw her off

Father's tower, not even a fever has assailed her. Instead, she simply faded away. Why?

I rise and gaze up, out of the window. Evening is coming and the stars are already glimmering faintly. Was it my fault? Was it because I no longer needed her?

Briseis and I became inseparable when I returned from the Bride Show. My six-year-old self arrived at the tower to find that I had been given the bed next to Pandora, as no-one wanted to associate with the eldest daughter after her disastrous snub at the hand of Empress Euphrosyne.

Briseis was already there, on the other side of my bed, on the other side of the high window, the only opening to give us any natural light. I surmised that in the scramble for beds, Briseis had come in nearly last, driven away from the shadows. Perhaps it was chance that brought us together. Perhaps it was fate. Briseis always relied on me, even though she was my elder by three years.

And now, as I look back along those ten long years of imprisonment, I realize how stuck everything has been. It is as if all of us have been suspended in ice, until Nobody appeared. As I began to rely on him more and more, Briseis faded into the background. As our feelings ripened, Briseis must have felt she no longer had any place in this world of ours. Has she willed her own death?

I cover my face with my hands and sob like a child. I don't know how long I remain like that until I feel an arm oh-so-gently slide around my shoulders and turn me. Soon enough I am weeping into the shoulder of a tall person, a tall male personage who is garbed in the softest of soft wool.

I raise my eyes.

Of course.

Nobody.

TWENTY-TWO

THE SLEEPING SICKNESS

Justice continues her story

Day after day I spend with my sisters in our round room at the top of the tower that has now become an infirmary of sorts. With three sisters dead, I must do everything in my power to help, for Maiden *Kore* is sick herself. She pricked her finger sewing strips of cloth into bandages, and now her finger is swollen and pulsating, an ugly reddish-purple color. Soon after, she slipped into a slumber that I cannot rouse her from.

The silence in our room is eerie as six of us ~ Helen *Shining*, Kore *Maiden*, Artemis *Bow*, Aphrodite *Sea-Foam*, Hecate *Ambiguity* and Chryseis *Treasure* ~ lie statue-still on their beds, only their faint breaths indicating they are still with us. I would have thrown myself down on my bed to slumber away my own exhaustion, had not Nobody told me it was so important to keep visiting my sisters one by one and talking with them.

"But they cannot hear me," I protest.

"You do not know that," he points out. "They do not *appear* to hear you. That doesn't mean that they don't hear you."

"But they are are asleep."

"Are they?" His grey eyes probe mine. Then he bows, and leaves, his absence causing tears to trickle down my cheek.

What is wrong with me? Angrily I swipe at my face, before rising and pacing around the room.

At least I have never-before-known privacy. Pandora spends her days on her knees in prayer, whether to Holy Mary or the goddess Athena, I cannot tell. Medusa spends her time with Father, running the court (and some say the country) on those days when he is present-but-absent. So, I have hours to ponder this new crush.

Why have I never felt this way before? *You've never been allowed to meet men,* remarks the voice in my head. But it is more than that. Nobody is not just any man. His presence makes me come alive. Something about him wakes me up. He makes me feel excited about life. Yes, I murmur to myself as the right word clicks into place, he *inspires* me.

For one thing, he is the cleverest person I have ever met. He has a strategy for everything. He takes a problem and breaks it down into smaller bite-sized pieces before examining every aspect of it. He lists options and considers them carefully too. He tells me that the best way to outthink an enemy is to be several steps ahead of them.

Every day, as I sit in a desultory fashion by one or another of my sister's beds, I await the soft sound of his footfall and feel my life-blood, usually so static, usually so dormant, rush to the surface, humming with energy, when he appears.

Is this a crush? Or is it something more? Is it love? I fold my arms around myself as I consider this. I cannot stop thinking about him. I obsess constantly over his words, every detail of the expressions that flit around that well-line face, every look and glance that come out of those penetrating grey eyes.

I flop onto my bed. How would I know? I've never been in love in my entire life. And I would know nothing about it were it not for my secret passion for reading. For on those nights that seem endless when sleep eludes me, I creep down those stairs, my bare feet sinking into the dew-encrusted lawn, as I wend my way to the Castle Library. I learned to make use of it during Morgana's tutelage, but now I go there for relaxation. My favorite volumes concern romance: Isabella and her Pot of Basil, Tristano and Isotta, Lancilotto and Ginevra.

My sisters have never had the opportunity to find love. All except Persephone *Death-Bringer*. I remember her radiant smile, as she gazed at her husband and baby. That is what love looks like. That is what I want. With Nobody.

Before I can chase another thought, I sink into a deep sleep.

When I awaken, Kore has gone. We bury her in the garden, near her favorite herbs.

TWENTY-THREE

The King's Command

Justice continues her story

As that long, warm Autumn melts into frosty Winter, when the great goddess dies a lingering death leaving behind her the flaming leaves that turn into dust, I tend to my remaining sisters, foregoing all sleep. For I can never forgive myself for not watching over Kore, for not taking her hand, nor holding her close during her last moments on this earth. I visit her grave every day, early in the morning before my sisters return.

They lie like pretty dolls during the day, waking up only as dusk comes on, the shimmering stars precipitating their departure. Every dawn they come back; their slippers ruined. As the evenings grow cooler, as the nights draw in, Father begins to take notice. He summons the shoemaker, and when the unfortunate man presents him with a long scroll detailing all the new slippers he has been making for the past several months, Father explodes.

"It is your daughters, sire," explains the man, doffing his cap and kneeling on the cold marble floor. "They wear out their slippers each night."

"Do you mean to tell me that *all* of my daughters have been dancing?"

"Not all of your daughters, sire. It is your younger daughters, and Lady Helen."

Father barks an order, but only Pandora, Medusa, and myself are able to appear, our other sisters being dead to the world.

"Well?" he roars.

"We don't know," we reply in unison.

"Don't know? he bellows. "What don't you know?"

As the silence lengthens, I step forward. "Father," I say, making a low curtsey before kneeling before him. "There are several things we don't know. We don't know what causes their sleeping sickness. We don't know why they sleep by day and go out at night. We don't know where they go. We don't even know why their slippers are ruined every night."

"Hmmm." Father strokes his beard.

I peer at him. He seems to be his usual self once more. Hope lightens in my bosom. If he can recover from his summer lethargy, perhaps my sisters can come back too.

"We must find out," remarks Father." He stands, his voice reverberating around the huge chamber, his Great Hall where he meets his magnates to discuss important affairs. "I am issuing a challenge to all young men in my kingdom. Whoever solves the puzzle of the ruined slippers, whoever finds out where my daughters go each night, that young man will marry my eldest daughter and rule this land after my death."

I glance at Pandora. As his courtiers rise to acclaim their King, she turns ashen-pale, collapsing onto the floor in a dead faint.

I awaken one morning to the sound of voices coming through the open window above my bed. Rolling out of bed, I gently place my stool on it so that I can clamber up to the window and peer out. The mists coil up from the river that surrounds our castle, making everything grey and hazy. I judge it to be that hour before dawn before the sun's tentacles throw beams of light across the dewy lawn, now that the cool weather is settling in.

Craning my neck, I see two figures below. One, of course, I recognize immediately. Nobody is already up, dressed in his soldier's garb of long boots, leather jerkin, leather braces, knives, sword, his shield slung over a short woolen cloak. The other figure is taller, but it is not until she speaks that I recognize her.

"Come now," my second sister Medusa says in that low growl she uses when trying to be seductive. "You know my elder sister is completely mad. If you marry me, my lord Nobody, you will rule this land."

He bows low and kisses her hand, far too slowly for my taste, for he kisses each knuckle, ending with her palm. "Lady Medusa," he murmurs.

Protectress, or *Medusa* (as I must now remember to call her), chuckles as a slow pinkness rises from her neck and spreads across her cheeks. The snakes sway languidly in the morning breeze.

"My lord," she purrs, or rather tries to purr - it emerges as another low growl - "How you do flatter me. Why I think you might even like me."

He gives another low bow and turns, proffering his arm, but staying out of range of her snakes. Now I can see the expression on his face. He seems—engrossed by Medusa, who is basking in his attention like a cat licking cream.

"We would make a fine pair, my lord," she is saying, smiling down at him. "For I am just as ambitious as you are, and you and I could become persons of great consequence. A power couple to make those lazy emperors up in Constantinople take notice. They will have to admit us to their councils."

He smiles up at her, eyes hooded.

"I don't know why you bother with that silly child, Justice," continues Medusa. "She has no ambition at all, no grit, no intelligence —."

Nobody interrupts at this point to say something, but their voices disappear as they round a corner.

I lean back from the window, nearly falling as I have forgotten that I am standing on a not-very-stable stool planted in the middle of my bed. Of course, Medusa would try to sink her claws into *my* suitor, for she has no suitor of her own. As the months have wound on, as our escape from Father seems ever further away, Medusa has become restless and impatient.

One thing only has not changed: five of our sisters still disappear every night, returning in the morning with ruined slippers. Father is running up a fortune in shoe leather and is not happy about it.

A week ago, he published his decree, asking all young men of rank and birth, all the heirs to the noble fortunes of this realm, to come to our palace and solve the mystery of the ruined slippers. The first one to win will marry the eldest daughter, my sorceress sister All-Gifted, now called *Lady Pandora*. No wonder Medusa is so restless. She would believe that *she* should be the prize. What will these young men think when they realize they are being wed to a thirty-year-old sorceress?

I slide off the bed and begin my morning rituals, plunging my hands into a bowl of icy water, washing my hair and face, dressing, and then doing my hair into a neat braid. What am I to make of Nobody's behavior? Why is he so entranced by Medusa? Surely, he can see her for the power-hungry monster she is.

I sit on my bed, reconsidering my decision to allow him to court me. Or rather my non-decision as he never actually asked me.

Do I really want to go through the ordeal of childbirth? I look down at my slender body.

How would I ever push out a baby? I would probably die in the attempt. Even if I survived, do I really want to go through all that agony only to experience the all-too-common heartbreak of losing a child to an early death?

Do I really expect Nobody to treat me well?

Do I really want the humiliation of being the forgotten wife?

And speaking of wives, who is Playful's mother?

And speaking of Playful, why haven't I seen him recently?

I pace the room, frowning. Is Playful sick too? Whatever has become of that charming boy with his mop of golden curls and grey eyes that are exactly like his father's?

And why is Nobody playing games? Why does he seem to be in Medusa's thrall? Whatever has happened that would cause him to choose her over me?

I sigh. What do I expect? Men bring nothing but trouble. He will treat me as badly as Pandora was treated at the Bride Show.

I fold my arms. I really *don't* want the companionship of any man. I will be safer and happier with my littlest sisters. And Pandora.

TWENTY-FOUR

PLAYFUL AND THE PEAR

Nobody speaks.

Things begin to go wrong when Playful comes to me one day. In one hand he holds a large pear, the color of bronze, which emanates a sinister glow.

I peer at it. Where does its light come from? Is it reflecting the rays of the rising sun?

"Father," he says, out of breath because he has run all the way from the castle, "what do I do?"

"Where did this come from?" I gesture to the magical object glowing softly in his hands.

"I don't know. I found it in the hayloft where I sleep with the other grooms."

"When?"

"Just now. I opened my eyes because I thought the sun was rising and I was already late. But it wasn't the sun. It was this. And now it won't leave me."

I frown. "What do you mean it won't leave you?"

"I can't put it down. It is stuck to my hand." He shows me, and indeed the pear solidly adheres to the palm side of his left hand.

"What should I do?" My thirteen-year-old boy, who has braved hiking across a strange country to come find me is close to tears.

I peer at it again, refraining from touching it. "There must be a task it wishes you to do."

"Yes."

I look up. "You know what it is."

He looks down, flushing. "I have to choose which sister is the fairest."

"Who gave you this task?" I ask, amused.

"Princess Helen," he mumbles.

"Ah yes. So, she left you this gift?"

He nods, his eyes glued to his feet. "I have to choose between all the sisters."

"So, you will choose her?"

"Probably."

"Why?"

My son's face crimsons, becoming so red that the tips of his ears crimson.

I gesture for him to sit.

It is a hot, autumnal day, he begins, his voice a thread of a whisper, *and the ladies are resting upstairs while I sit alone, in the main hall strumming my lyre. The sun is not quite overhead, which means I still have time before visiting you. Those hot mornings hang heavy on my hands because the heat makes the ladies lethargic, not stirring from their beds until noon.*

A swish of silks makes me look up, and there stands the most beautiful lady I have ever seen. She has waist-length golden hair that curls around her shoulders. She has a line of black around her eyes which makes them seem enormous. Her eyes are green, a deep green color I've never seen before that reminds me of curling ferns, secret nooks, or dank ponds. One eye has a fleck in it, the color of an orange.

She stands in the doorway, her hands on either side of the door, blocking any hope of escape. A sudden breeze rises, making her white silken gown ripple.

He stops, going even more crimson.

"And?" I prompt.

"I lower my eyes, trying not to notice the black triangle between her legs," he whispers even more softly.

I chuckle in the back of my throat. "So, Princess Helen - the bold, naughty sister who favors translucent gowns - appeared for a visit?"

My son nods, clenching his hands together. He doesn't smile.

"What happened next?"

"She talked to me."

"What did she say?"

"She called me *Pretty Boy*. There was something about the way she said it that made the hairs rise on the back of my neck." My son tilts his head up. "She had a low husky voice that seemed somehow both inviting and threatening."

"Interesting," I murmur, struck by his powers of observation. My son, after all, is only a thirteen-year-old boy.

I wait, but there is a long pause, almost as if my son is picking and choosing what to tell me.

"Just say it," I remark eventually.

He looks up. *She comes forward, putting forth a talon-like finger. I flinch as she tilts my chin, forcing me to look into those ocean-like eyes.*

"We are alone," she purrs.

I stiffen.

"Come," she holds out a hand.

I remain, clutching my lyre to my belly.

She laughs. "I don't scratch!"

"But—but your nails." They are long and white, extending the length of her fingers by a knucklebone.

She laughs again. "Have you never seen expertly manicured nails?" She holds them up for me to inspect. They are flawless, each nail the exact same shape as its sister. There is a slight gold dusting on them that makes them glint in the sun.

"It must take hours to do that," I say.

"It passes the time," she replies with a sigh.

I peer up at her. "What have you done to your eyes?"

"Why don't you come to my room, and I'll show you?"

I clutch my lyre, my spine suddenly tingling. *What is wrong with me? Why shouldn't I go to the pretty lady's room?*

Slowly, I put my lyre down and take her hand.

She takes me up an interminable twisting stairway, which gives out just outside a large round room. For such a large room, there should be plenty of space but it is crammed with beds, dressers, stools, and possessions. I count. There are eight beds. Of course, four of the sisters are dead.

I shiver. This sister looks remarkably like Princess Clytemnestra - the sister who fell from the tower - except she had blue eyes, not green.

Princess Helen sits down at one of the tables, covered with pots and brushes of various sizes, and slowly and delicately makes up my face. By the time she's finished, I have those black lines around my eyes, which curve up to a flourish on the outside where the lid meets the rest of the face. I have unnaturally white skin, unnaturally pink cheeks, and red lips that would put a tart to shame.

I try not to grimace as I stare at myself in her overly large mirror. She has made me look like a whore.

"Do you like it?" She purrs.

I hate it, but how can I tell her that?

"Perhaps something different?"

I glance out the window and notice the sun is overhead.

I rise, but her claw-like hand clamps down on my wrist, forcing me to sit. "Why the hurry?"

I look around. The door is ajar. All I need do is get there. I will have to be quick so that I can escape before she can do anything about it.

I shove away from her and rise.

"Don't you want to try more looks?"

I make for the door.

"Come back!" She moves toward me.

"Father will be waiting," I stammer out.

I just have time to see her raise a brow before I hurl myself down the stairs.

"Your father is *here*?" Her voice rises on the last word.

She comes to the door. "Don't you want me to wipe your makeup off?" She calls down the stairs. "What is your father going to think?"

Her voice reverberates down those stone stairs as I tumble down, my breath coming out in puffs. I know I must look ridiculous, but I cannot get away from her fast enough.

I run as fast as I can, once I reach the bottom of the stairs. But I am not fast enough.

My son stops, seized by a fit of coughing.

I bang him on the back, offering my ale.

The silence, once he has finished drinking, is deafening.

"You were discovered, sometime later, by the guards?"

He nods, his face flaming again.

"She was naked?"

"We were both naked," he whispers.

I lean back against the wall of the stable, fury uncoiling in my belly. "Your first time?"

He nods.

"She made you—"

He nods again. "It was her cries that attracted attention. I thought she was in pain, but—"

"She wasn't," I finish for him.

My son looks down, his face as red as a poppy.

"Sooo." I let out a long breath. "She enticed you to play a game you did not care to play?"

Playful looks straight at me. "What happens now?" He tries to wipe the sweat off his face, but that damn pear makes it difficult for him to move his left hand.

"I will go with you to the tower room," I say, "and you will pick her as the fairest out of all her remaining sisters so you can get rid of that dangerous plaything. Once that is done, I will have words with her."

"But—but won't she send me to the dungeons?"

I frown. My boy seems unnaturally scared. "Kousaleos," I say, using his formal Greek name, "I can handle manipulative women."

TWENTY-FIVE

THE MARRIAGE PLEDGE

Callidice speaks

Where is he?

Where is *my* so-called admirer?

Slowly, I roll out of bed into the cold embrace of an early winter dawn and look around. Pandora is snoring heavily, as is her custom. Next to her is Medusa.

I frown at Medusa's slumbering form. I thought *he* was wooing her, but now that I think of it, she has been sullen these past few days, rousing herself to snap peevishly at whoever gets in her way. Her snakes mirror her mood, lethargic with sudden bursts of energy, their tongues flickering in and out.

She was particularly vicious to Helen the other day—

I gaze absently as the sky lightens. Helen. Where is she? I stand by the door, my chin lifted, waiting.

As the sun's rays throw beams of light high into the sky, they appear— Chryseis, her golden curls gnarled in tangles, Hecate holding a torch aloft, Aphrodite limping, Artemis scowling.

"Where is Helen?"

They creep by me, their eyes down, except Hecate who looks directly at me. "Do you not know?"

My stomach sinks. "Where?" I whisper.

"In the stables."

I raise a brow. I cannot imagine Helen conducting a love affair surrounded by tickling straw and horse dung, but—Before another thought arises, I run. I run as fleet as a hare. I run until I find them.

But they are not in a lover's embrace. *At least, not now* I tell myself. Nobody is sitting on a bale of hay dousing a lantern. Next to him, wide-eyed and terrified is his son Playful. Helen, glamorous in a shimmering gown, pouts as the lantern light dies, rendering her dress dullish in the dimness of the barn.

I search Nobody's face. His lines are more deeply etched than usual, his frown cutting furrows in his forehead. He looks at Helen, his grey eyes steely, his lips hardening.

"That is all you have to say?"

Even Helen flinches at the coldness of his tone.

"I hold you responsible," he grinds out. "If anything should happen to my son—"

"You'll kill me?" she replies in a husky voice.

I stare at her. How can she be so flippant in the face of his fury?

He glares at her.

She giggles. But her eyes give her away. My sister is not jesting. She fears Nobody.

He continues to glare. The silence lengthens, stretches, becoming unbearably taut. Just when I think I cannot bear it anymore, Helen abruptly turns on her heel, disappearing in a swirl of silk.

He catches sight of me as I move out of the shadows, his face softening. "My love! My

Beautiful Justice! My Callidice!" He takes my hand and kisses it, nuzzling each knuckle, ending with a kiss on the palm which he gently closes with my fingers.

My cheeks heat causing the tips of my ears to burn. For Playful is no longer looking wide-eyed and terrified, but wide-eyed and amused. Fortunately, his good manners hold him in check, because instead of a derisive laugh, only one corner of his mouth twitches.

I turn to Nobody. What do I say? I haven't seen him in over a week. The rhythm of our relationship has been lost.

He gestures for me to sit beside him. "You are wondering what has happened."

How well he reads me.

"I have been trying to solve a difficult knot of a problem—"

"What problem?"

"I really cannot say," he remarks looking me straight in the eye. Behind him, Playful flushes crimson.

I purse my lips into a thin line. "You can trust me."

He leans forward and pats my knee. "Dearest," he says. "Of course, I trust you."

"But *not* about this matter."

"This is extremely—delicate. It concerns the reputations of people who are close to you."

"You mean my sisters?"

He looks away.

I fold my arms. "What exactly have you been saying to Medusa?"

He is silent.

"*She* believes you to be her suitor. I hear that she has great plans to rule this kingdom with *you* and cut such a swash amongst the Kingly Rulers that you will both be admitted to the Highest Councils in Constantinople."

He stares at me, a faint flush creeping up his cheeks.

"You intend to marry her!" I explode.

"I do not," he replies evenly.

"You lie!" I shout. "I saw you in the garden with her—"

"You misunderstand—"

"What is there to misunderstand? It must be clear to you that Medusa will take power. Who in their right mind would want to marry a thirty-year-old sorceress who looks old before her time?"

"And what prince in his right mind would want to marry a power-hungry murderess?" he counters.

I stop, staring at him.

He strokes tendrils of hair away from my face, easing his thumb over my tear-streaked cheeks. "My love," he says gently. "Let us consider the situation calmly. You are right about your eldest sister, and I am right about your second sister. Your third sister, Queen Persephone, is married and belongs in the Underworld. That leaves—"

"Helen!" I interrupt. "What about her?"

His lips thin. "What do you take me for? I am a rational man. Why would I yoke myself to a strumpet who will embarrass me at every turn?"

Again, I still. "I'm sorry," I murmur.

He kisses my hand. "Your fifth sister Princess Kore, and your sixth sister Princess Briseis are not longer with us."

I look down. "Kore would have made a good wife," I whisper.

"You are probably right," he concedes. "However, I do not think she cared for men."

I look up. He misses nothing

"Your sixth sister, Princess Briseis would have found it too overwhelming to be my wife and to rule a kingdom with me."

Tears fill my eyes. Shadow was so fragile, always had been. Even when I was a young child, I cared for her.

He smiles. "However, the seventh sister, you, my darling Callidice, are perfection." His lips meet mine.

Immediately, I melt, warmth radiating from the very center of my being. Just as he deepens his kiss, I put a hand on his chest and gently pull away. Looking deep into his eyes, I say "You cannot marry me, or anyone."

"My wife is dead," he replies immediately, a shade too swift.

I frown. How I long to say *prove it*, but that is ridiculous. How could he possibly do that? He is probably hundreds of miles from home.

Later, I wonder. Has he lied to me? I am almost sure he has. Or perhaps he just does not know. After all, that war took ten years to fight. Then there is the journey home. By my calculations, he hasn't seen his wife in *fourteen years*. Of course, she could be dead. *But what if she isn't?* asks the voice in my head. *What then?* I frown and huff out a sigh. What is wrong with me?

An icy moon rises silently above the tall trees of the garden. Out of the corner of my eye, I glimpse a flutter of white. It is Helen in one of her white dresses, newly embroidered (by me) with tiny disks of gold that cause it to shimmer in the half-light of dusk. With her is Nobody.

They lean together, talking in low voices. Her hand strokes his bare arm. She lifts her face as if to kiss when suddenly I take myself by surprise and stride forward. I pinch my lips to contain the vat of fury that roils my belly.

"I require a rational man," I say, my voice as sharp as the edge of a newly-forged blade. "Throughout my life, I have searched diligently for such a Paragon. Unfortunately, I have not had the good fortune to come across him."

Nobody stares at me, his steel eyes darkening with interest. Then he gives a sharp bark of laughter, dropping Helen's hand as it if were a hot coal from the oven. Coming forward, he flourishes a low bow.

"My Lady Callidice well met. Am I to understand that my failings have just disqualified me from becoming your husband?"

Before I can tell him that yes, he has failed miserably, Helen strides to his side. "*Husband?*" she shrills. "You are going to marry *her*?"

He favors her with a cold glance. "Of course, I am going to marry Callidice."

Helen's face is a picture. "But—but I don't get it. I am the loveliest woman in the world —"

"Not according to that dangerous game you made my son play." He bares his teeth as he comes closer to her. "Lady Helen, you didn't win that contest with the magical pear, your half-sister Aphrodite won."

"But Aphrodite is just a child," she sputters, "only thirteen."

"Nevertheless, all the princes concurred in this grave matter." His voice lingers on the word *grave* to coat it with a sarcastic edge. "Surely you don't mean to disagree with the judgments of Hades, King of the Underworld, or his Gatekeeper, Lord Charon, or Ares, Lord War, Osiris, Lord Afterlife, Zeus, Lord Deity, or even the goddess Athena?"

Helen's face turns purple. I have never seen her so furious. "How dare you disrespect me—"

Nobody folds his arms. "Why not? You are a strumpet, a harlot, a whore. Why would any rational man want *you* as his wife?"

"Ooooh." Helen's face clears. "That is why Callidice talked about your being rational—"

"Indeed. And that is precisely why I love and respect her." He takes my hand and kisses it. "Lady Callidice," he proclaims, holding my hand high, "is the most interesting young woman I have ever met." His eyes fall into mine as he kneels. "Lady Helen, I call upon you to witness my undying love for your sister Lady Callidice. I hope that one day she will consent to be my wife."

My cheeks flame. Suddenly I cannot bear it, the silken softness of his eyes, the poisonous fury emanating from Helen, the murderous rage that Medusa will surely send my way. I drop his hand and flee—like a child. Something propels me into the forests surrounding the castle, where, with a power I did not know I possessed, I climb the tallest tree I can find, crouching in its fork until my heart stops its hammering, my hands their shaking, my eyes their weeping.

I am only sixteen years old, unused to the world of men and their machinations. I wipe my eyes with my sleeve as I slow my breath. How like a man to make a perilous situation even more poisonous. I should be delighted, I know. What young woman would not want the respect of a brilliant man who is twice her age? What woman would not want a man who fascinates her to proclaim his undying love, especially in front of the sister who had been the focus of so much jealousy? *But what does he really want?* niggles the voice in the back of my mind. *Is it going to be what you want?*

I sigh and look down through the branches as the moon's cold shimmer penetrates the thick foliage around me. The question should be what do *I* really want?

TWENTY-SIX

THE EXECUTIONS OF THE SUITORS

Callidice speaks

Months pass sluggishly as winter blossoms into spring. I pass through, suspended, my choice balanced on a knife's edge, avoiding Nobody. The man sucks the air out of the room. A flick of his glance pierces through me while my heart dances like a giddy girl drunk on her first cup of wine. I cannot think in his presence, and so I keep to myself.

The good weather brings the first suitors to our castle who crawl over the castle battlements, and peer into hidden corners, even into our round chamber. Finally, Father posts guards at our door when he catches a couple of them fingering our finery—and our *underclothes*.

But instead of shutting us in, behind the swords, the shields, and the smirks of his armed guards, Father allows us to go outside. We are given fine gowns, golden chains for our necks and to thread through our hair, earrings, bracelets, bangles, necklaces, rings. Even pets. All those things he had forgotten to lavish on his daughters these many years.

Why Father changed his mind, Heaven knows. I thought him too mean to bother finding husbands for us. But perhaps his decree had the unintended consequence of shining a light on his twelve neglected daughters. For some said our frenzied dancing and our ruined slippers are a cry for help. Was Father embarrassed?

We react in different ways to this sudden change. After too many visits from suitors eager to claim her hand, Pandora finally covers her face and hair in ashes, ensuring her invisibility as she bows over her cauldron muttering spells.

The suitors turn to Medusa, believing her to be the eldest. But perhaps Medusa's snakes put them off, for as soon as Helen appears, one curve of her seductive lips brings them to heel. We can always tell where Helen is nowadays as she is surrounded by a bevy of men, whose deep voices bounce off the castle walls, whose boots trample not only the hard-packed surfaces of the yard, but the lush green lawns of the gardens, and even Father's prized flowers. News of Helen must spread like wildfire for the men keep appearing ~ twelve, twenty-four, forty-eight. By the time we are hosting seventy-two of them, Father puts his foot down and many hopeful young men are turned away at the gates.

With the death-marriages of Persephone and Intrigue, and the vanishing of Briseis and Kore, I am next on their list after Helen. After me, is Artemis. But she is too much of a hoyden, so that even though at fourteen she is actually ready to marry, she is invisible to the young men. They probably think she is a kitchen wench. Thirteen-year-old Aphrodite casts a mysterious allure, but she is a young-looking thirteen, while twelve-year-old

Hecate is just plain mysterious to them. No-one is looking for a five-year-old bride, and so Chryseis escapes their notice. Thus, none of us can match Helen for her power to compel.

When our father the King sent his message out to all the young men in the kingdom, inviting them to come and help him solve the puzzle of the ruined slippers, he promised that the victor would marry his eldest daughter and rule the kingdom with her after his death. But what most young men didn't realize amidst their joy at the King's invitation, unless they cast their eyes all the way to the bottom of this very long scroll, was that those who failed would die.

Seventy-two come, *all* die.

Father enjoys executing them in various ways.

If he knows the young man personally, that young man is allowed to fall onto his sword.

If the young man is high-born, but not known to him personally, he is beheaded by an expert swordsman.

If the young man is low-born, but has shown courage and dignity when receiving his death sentence, he is hanged.

Those unfortunate young men who challenged his authority, the entitled, the drunk, and the despised are treated to the torments of wild beasts, vats of burning oil, vats of molten gold, molten silver, or molten bronze. In these cases, Father makes a celebration out of each death, humiliating the victim in public, before turning on his heel and leaving each to his cruel fate.

Everyone is invited to watch, especially his daughters. Medusa is always there, seated by Father's side as lady of the land, rejoicing in the humiliations and cruel fates of these unfortunate suitors as much as Father.

I never attend. Instead (as Father isn't paying attention), I take my younger sisters outside, away from the shouts, the laughs, the groans, the screams, and the stench. We take a picnic and roam the forests around the castle all day long, only coming back at nightfall after the last victim is long gone.

Sometimes Pandora leaves her cauldron to join us. Occasionally Helen accompanies us on our country rambles, although she is too eager to wrest the title of Father's favorite daughter away from Medusa to come frequently.

During this time, Nobody attends each and every killing. When I see him with Playful, I challenge him about it.

"I am a soldier," he remarks.

"But what about your son?"

He grips my arm. "Why have you been avoiding me?"

I look up into a pair of icy grey eyes. "I haven't been avoiding you."

His grip tightens. "Do not lie to me," he hisses. "You led me on. You let me believe you loved me as much as I love you. Then you drop me like a stone in your shoe."

My cheeks heat. "I didn't mean—" I falter. *What can I possibly say?*

"You are a prick-tease," he spits. "I thought the world of you, and now I see you are a strumpet, just like your sister."

I pull my arm away. "I am *not* like Helen," I whisper, my cheeks now heating with fury. "Surely you will allow me to have doubts. I am only sixteen. I have lived my entire life in a prison. I know little about men, or queenship, or motherhood. What do you expect me to do? I need more time."

"You've had months," he counters.

I draw myself up. "I am a princess." My voice is cold. "I am expected to make a splendid match. Father has been parading me in front of every man in this kingdom. Do you really think I have any say in this matter?"

His eyes soften, as he kisses my hand.

"Why didn't *you* present yourself before Father as one of our suitors?" I ask.

He flushes. "You know I cannot do that."

"Why not?" I tilt my head up so that I can gaze into his eyes. "Your wife is dead."

There is silence.

"Your wife is *not* dead."

He presses his lips together. "I did not say that."

"No, you did not," I agree. "But you haven't denied it either."

"Mother is alive." Playful emerges from the shadows. "Or at least she was when last I saw her—two years ago."

"So, she could be dead," remarks Nobody.

I glare at him as I wrench my hand away. "You think so little of your wife you will *not* make any attempt to keep your marriage vows?"

He throws back his head and laughs. Then he takes my hand and kisses it again.

I frown up at him. "What is so funny?"

"Your innocence," he replies, smiling down at me. "You know so little of men."

I take a step back. "I already told you that. And what I see, I don't much care for."Before he can reply, I turn on my heel and leave.

TWENTY-SEVEN

THE CORPSE

Callidice speaks

With the suitors all dead, there is no man alive to free us. Outside, the Sikelian spring creates its loveliest colors, its most tempting aromas, its trilling birdsong, all against a backdrop of dazzling days and serene nights. But inside our round chamber we eight princesses sink into sorrow. Pandora ceases her spells. Medusa and Helen slide into torpor, while Artemis, Aphrodite, Hecate and Chryseis lie motionless on their beds, their slippers shiny and new as they have ceased dancing. I am the only one who continues her duties, embroidering in the morning, plain sewing in the afternoon. In between I am up and down those stairs, bringing refreshments for my sisters from the kitchens, so that they won't fade away completely.

Thus, during a blur of uneventful days as searing winds beget the summer heat, I hear Cook remark that we have arrived at May Day Eve, that time when the veil between this world and the next thins, when the souls of the dead come alive to visit those dear ones left behind. And so, I determine that I will follow my sisters to see if I can solve the puzzle of the ruined slippers, as I am sure they will arise tonight. I spend sleepless hours watchful, vigilant, until that hour when night has rolled in.

A faint movement catches the edge of my vision, and the spiral pattern appears in the middle of the floor. Slowly, it spirals around, unfurling a set of spiral stairs. One by one, my sisters stir to descend those stairs. Even Pandora and Medusa arise from their beds to plunge into that utter darkness.

I am the last to leave.

Slowly, I move down the shallow steps, hearing the floor-door grind shut behind me.

It is nine months since I last was here and everything seems just as it was before. Once the door is shut, the smooth walls of the tunnel come alive with torches placed at intervals. The cold freshness of the night air assails us as we leave the tunnel, plucking us out of our torpor. The narrow path between the runnel and a high wall wends its way downhill as the runnel transforms itself into a stream that becomes a roaring waterfall. The jewel trees, the lake, the boats and the princes: all are the same as before.

The princes are tall, dark-haired, clad in black, courteous and anonymous behind their black masks. Except for one of them, an individual who is much shorter and sports a mop of fair curls. I peer at him. Surely, it cannot be. Surely Nobody's son Playful is not *here*?

But before I can stop her, Helen grabs his hand, leading him to the fourth boat. Slowly, I take in the sight before me. There are twelve boats, just as before, but the third, fifth, sixth, and eighth are empty. As we glide across the lake, they glide with us, propelled by some unseen power.

And now that I think about it, this place of the In-Between *is* different from before. Where is Lord Charon, Clytemnestra's husband? Where are the slithering creatures that accompanied us on our first journey through the tunnel? Where are the birds who perched in the jeweled trees? Gilgamesh, the Dragon-Men, Persephone, Kore, Briseis, and Clytemnestra? The silence is profound.

And when we arrive at the castle, its white marble glowing in the hundreds of candles that have been set around and about it, yet there is no sound. We arise from our boats, gliding across the marble floor as we dance noiselessly all night long.

We arise in the late afternoon, our slippers torn, our temples pounding, our eyes crusted up with an unnatural sleep. The seven of us perform our toilettes, washing our faces and arms, applying ointments to our faces and necks, combing out our hair and dressing it, pulling on our garments, adorning ourselves with necklaces, earring, brooches, bracelets, and rings. Finally, my gaze latches onto something. No, not something but someone. And not a personage but the *absence* of one such.

Where is Helen?

Suddenly, I rise to my feet, pushing away my unusual lethargy and hurry down the stairs. Someone must have drugged the wine, and even now the coils of that poison interfere with my ability to focus. As I emerge into the garden I hear a sound.

"No!" A roar comes from the Great Hall.

I run, stopping suddenly as I arrive, my eyes adjusting to the dimness. The fire in the fire-pit is smoking, tendrils of smoke coiling into the still air, creating a smoke-screen.

I can make out only vague shapes as the cats slide off into the shadows, the dogs bark, and the people part to let me through.

"No!" The sound reverberates around the huge hall, a wounded beast in its death throes.

As I arrive at the thrones, I peer at a large shape bent over something.

"No! Not my son!"

I rush forward to see Nobody kneeling on the polished marble floor, tears gushing down his face, a headless corpse flung across his knees, blood oozing everywhere.

I have never seen anyone so distraught. Nobody's muscular frame shudders with each sob, each guttural cry, as he cradles this mass of tissue, bone, and blood in his arms. I sink to my knees heedless of the blood soaking my robes, as I too-slowly realize that this is what is left of his son Playful. Idly, I wonder if this boy was his heir, his only son, or if there is another back home.

My heart twists as I take in his ravaged face. I haven't seen him in months and now I wonder why. Why have I been so unkind to this man? All difficulties fade as I take in his devastation. He is the only sane person in this viperish hell-hole that we sisters have yet to escape.

"What are you so upset about, my lord?"

Father's voice rips me out of my thoughts. I look up. He has risen from his throne, a wine cup in one hand, a sword in the other.

"I treated your puny rat-faced boy as an aristocrat."

Nobody surges to his feet, lunging at Father, another bellow erupting from his throat.

The guards grab his arms, dragging him away.

"My son! My son! My son! My son!" My heart twists as his cries gradually fade into the distance.

I glance at Father. His robes are bathed in blood. His sword drips blood. There is blood spattering his face and his hands.

I sink to my knees, vomiting over and over until there is nothing left. Father is out of control. He is cruel. He is power-mad. Someone must stop him.

I stand, wiping my mouth with the back of my hand.

Now that Nobody has been caged, that someone is going to be me.

TWENTY-EIGHT

MURDER

Nobody speaks

I first notice something wrong when my son fails to appear one afternoon. It is that time of day when sleep takes hold of everyone, when my son would appear and we would share a simple meal of cheese, bread, olive oil, and figs.

Although Kousaleos is small for his age and often looks younger, in many ways my boy behaves more responsibly than many a thirteen-year-old. So by the time the sun has drifted halfway down to the place where it vanishes for several hours, I grow concerned.

Where could he be?

Abandoning my tasks as stable-hand, I walk through the warm air of a spring afternoon to the castle. When I arrive, everything is quiet. Too quiet. I shiver despite the warmth. This is not the peaceful quiet of a sleepy afternoon, but something with a menacing edge.

Softly, I make my way to the Great Hall, and there everyone is. But instead of the rumblings of conversation punctuated by barks of laughter and the occasional shout, the multitude gathered there on that warm afternoon is silent. Too silent.

Peering through the gloom of the smoky interior I can make out King Euphemius seated on his throne. Next to him sits Medusa, whose expression is very different from her usual scowl. Now, a smile curves her lips and her eyes gleam in the lamplight making her look almost attractive.

She leans forward as if to say something, and then I see it.

Him.

Kousaleos.

My son.

Without thinking I surge forth, striding towards the dais.

Silently, the soldiers, the men-at-arms, the hangers-on, and the female slaves who do the household chores part to let me through.

I arrive at the dais, my fury as hot as a molten shaft of bronze, ready to be hammered into a deadly spear.

Medusa lifts her head and gazes at me. "Ah!" she says. "Your father has come for you after all."

I look at my son. His face is ashen, his eyes wide, and one tear slowly leaks down his cheek. I can see that he is struggling to act like a man, struggling to quell his fear so that he stands tall, squaring his shoulders and lifting his chin, just as I had taught him. But it is the expression in his eyes that chill the very marrow of my bones. They look haunted, mask-like, dead.

I turn to the King. "What are you doing to my son?"

The King waves a hand as if he is brushing away a fly. "He must play by the rules, as all others have before him."

"What are you talking about?"

"He lost," replies King Euphemius.

"Lost what?"

"I see you do not understand, my lord," purrs Medusa. "For you are not a stable hand are you, but the King of Ithaca?"

I clench my jaw. I have tried so hard to be anonymous at this court because I don't trust King Euphemius to treat his royal guests with the proper hospitality due to their rank. To be plain, I fear I would be held hostage - yet again - by a King whose madness I cannot yet gauge.

Medusa laughs softly. "Oh, my lord," she sighs clasping her bejeweled hands together. "You thought yourself so very clever did you not? You never thought that some might wonder why an illustrious King might spend his nights berthed in a manger? It never occurred to you that it was so very obvious you'd come to spy on us?"

She rises to her feet and points a finger at me. "You," she proclaims, her voice reverberating around that too-quiet-room, "are the wily Odysseus, Creator of the Trojan Horse—"

"What is going on?" My voice cuts like a sword.

"Ah yes, your son," she purrs again. "Charming little Playful whose real name is Prince Kousaleos of Ithaca. Well, he decided to play suitor, so that he could marry one of us princesses and claim the throne of Sikelia from Father." She strokes Kousaleos' cheek with a finger.

He flinches.

"Such a pretty boy," she coos. "Such a pity —"

"And?"

"Well, of course, the poor boy failed." She turns to me. "I made sure of that by giving him a cup of wine last night, just as I did for *all* of our suitors."

I grab her arm. "You bitch!" I spit. "You mean you were responsible for *all* their deaths?"

"Of course," she trills out, laughing.

"But why?"

"WHY?" She screams. She turns to the crowd. "He asks *why*?" She turns back to me. "Why would *I* want a husband? Why would *I* want to give *my* castle, *my* lands, *my* jewels, *my* clothes, and *my* body over to someone else? Why would *I* want to die before my time in the throes of childbirth? Of course, I made very sure that *all my* suitors died. It was a *pleasure* to watch." Her laughter verges on the edge of hysteria. "As for your boy, why would *I* want a puny brat who does not know how to satisfy a woman—"

I backhand her across the cheek so hard that her head snaps to one side and she falls to her knees.

By the time she composes herself, I am surrounded by a ring of men, and she is holding her swollen cheek and glaring.

"Guards!" she shouts.

Immediately, two of them grab my boy.

"No!" I yell. And before thought, my sword is out of its sheath, and I am laying about me. I don't know how many men I kill before I see a silver flash in the corner of my eye. Kousaleos' head plops onto the floor, blood pouring everywhere, coiling around my bare feet, making the marble floor viscous and sticky.

"NOOOOH!" I roar, as the guards grab me and wrap me in chains. "NOOOOH!" I roar over and over again as they drag me down to the dungeons.

"But why are you so upset, my lord?" calls King Euphemius after me. "I gave your boy an aristocrat's death, more than he deserved. Why, I beheaded him myself. I used my sharpest sword. The child didn't feel a thing —"

At length, we arrive at the stinking underground dungeons. I sink to my knees in filthy straw as the gate clangs shut.

After that, a blessed oblivion descends.

TWENTY-NINE

SORROW

Odysseus speaks

I don't know how long I lie there. It could have been a day; it could have been a week. At length, I hear the scrape of iron upon iron, the jangle of chains and the door opens. I shield my eyes from the unaccustomed blare of light.

A figure stands in the doorway, a figure whose face I cannot see, hidden beneath the shade of a large hood. I peer more closely. Is this Medusa, come to gloat? But the figure is too slender, bereft of the hissing snakes. Is this Helen, come to seduce me? But the figure emanates quietude, totally unlike the ploys of a strumpet. As I continue to gaze, a deep calm washes over me. Whatever happens now, I am in a better place than before. Eventually, the figure throws off her cloak and I see Callidice gazing at me, eyes thoughtful.

"I should have come sooner," she remarks. "No-one has dressed your wounds."

The open door fills my cell with the blazing light of the sun. For the first time I am able to study my body and see that indeed, I am covered in bruises, welts, cuts, and gashes. Some of these are an angry red.

"What day is it?"

She names a day that is ten days later than my boy's death.

"Ten days," I say.

She flushes. "I could not come."

"You mean your father forbade it."

She is silent.

"And you always listen to your father."

She remains silent.

I cock my head, studying her closer. In the year since we first met, I have seen her in many different moods, charming, merry, jealous, angry, and enraged. I expect my last barb to bring anger to her cheeks. But she remains still, as if my words don't matter.

Does she even care for me? Is she completely indifferent? Or does she wish to punish me? But as I gaze at those clear grey eyes, I understand that she hasn't come here to hurt me. She wishes to help.

I look down at my feet. They are crusted with dirt and dried blood. My clothes reek. My hair is matted. I stink of ordure. How I wish I were in my finest clothes. For I haven't seen her to talk to in oh-so-long, and I realize how much I've missed her company. What was the last thing we talked about? I sigh, searching those evanescent threads of memory. Of course. It was about my wife. I close my eyes, hoping that Penelope's face will come back to me. But the memory is so faint. Is Penelope dead, or alive? I hold still, hoping that Apollo or one of the gods will give me an answer. But nothing comes.

"I have to respect my father's wishes." Her voice is cool. "He could lock me up. Again."

I raise my head. "What makes today different?"

"I put poppy juice into his wine."

For the first time in a long while, I smile.

An answering smile curves the corners of her lips. "We don't have an endless amount of time." She nods and two guards enter. I slip into oblivion as they remove my chains.

When finally I awaken, my head is encased in bandages, my wrists are surrounded by sweet-smelling poultices and my legs have been wrapped in cool linens.

Slowly, oh-so-slowly, I heft myself into a sitting position, trying to ignore the the protests of my legs.

"Nobody!" She rushes forward. "You mustn't do that; you will hurt yourself."

"I can manage," I mutter as the room begins to tilt.

"No, you cannot," she returns, her voice low and authoritative. "You may be King of Ithaca, but you cannot do impossibilities." She bends over to rearrange the fine linen sheets, topped by a striped woolen blanket, staring into my eyes all the while.

"Why didn't you tell me who you were?"

I sigh. "I didn't trust your father."

She sits down beside my bed and folds her hands. "But don't you think it would have been better to introduce yourself to all of us honestly?"

I remain silent. Everything is hazy and my memories so faint. What was I doing? Why wasn't I honest? *If you'd been honest, your son would still be alive,* remarks the voice in my head.

"The trouble with hiding from all of us is that no-one knows whether to trust you or not." A corner of her mouth tugs up. "I admit that the name *Nobody* was a brilliant touch, Odysseus. But I would much rather have known who you really were."

I close my eyes. Everything seems too much now. Even thinking about my many past schemes gives me a headache. And where had it left me? King Euphemius the Mad had murdered my boy. My sour stomach clenches. The loss of my boy is like poison running through my veins.

"What have you been doing here?"

Her voice draws me out of my thoughts. I open my eyes expecting to fall into a scowl. Yet her grey eyes are remarkably serene. "Trying to gather more information about you and your sisters."

"Why?"

I sigh. *Why indeed? Why hadn't I gone on my way? What kept me here?* But one glance at her face gives me my answer.

"So, you are a spy," she remarks conversationally, as if she were talking about the weather.

"Not exactly." I draw in a deep breath. "I was interested in *you*."

"You mean you were interested in whether an alliance with Father would help the Kingdom of Ithaca." Her voice is cold.

I heft myself up again to protest her very reasonable suggestion, when my legs object and again I wince.

"Lie still," she snaps, as she re-arranges a pillow behind my head. It feels glorious.

"Yes, my lady," I reply.

The corner of her mouth twitches.

I decide to take advantage of her levity. At least it will distract me from thinking about my son. "How are things? Or perhaps I shouldn't ask."

A gust of laughter bursts out of her as she sags onto a seat. My gaze sweeps around the room and I realize I have been brought to that round chamber at the top of the Princesses' Tower.

"Things are peaceful now," she breathes out. "For Father is no longer with us."

"How?"

She lowers her eyes. "Someone put too much poppy juice in his wine."

"And that someone was you?"

She looks directly at me. "Does it matter?"

I smile and shake my head. "You did it for me. To avenge Playful."

Answering tears trickle down her cheeks.

There is a long pause.

"Where are Medusa and Helen?" I say eventually.

She looks at her hands folded in her lap.

"Hidden?" I suggest.

She looks up and our eyes meet.

Her expression emanates a depth of sorrow I have not seen before. Her lovely face is sunk with weariness as if she is already so tired of this life. Her clothes are wrinkled, her hair is coming loose from her plaits, and her eyes are surrounded by dark shadows. *Why isn't she resting? Has she been spending every hour of the day and night nursing me?*

If only I had more to offer her. I am King of Ithaca, yes, but I have little with me. Only three changes of clothes and some coin for my journey. I have not seen Ithaca in fourteen years, and who knows whether I still rule that land. Callidice needs a real husband, not some fool twice her age who is possibly married. Someone needs to stay and rule this kingdom with her. How I wish I could help.

I look around the round room with its beds and feminine articles - clothes, potions, looms, spindles - strewn everywhere.

"Where are your sisters?"

"Pandora has finally come back to us and taken on the task of educating our younger sisters. She is teaching them penmanship, arithmetic, rhetoric, and herbal medicine."

"That is an interesting combination of skills."

"She thinks they should become healers, but excellent healers have to deal with difficult people. Especially male aristocrats." She slides her eyes towards me. "Pandora thinks they should know the art of arguing."

"I could help," I offer.

A smile reluctantly blooms on her face. She lowers her eyes. "I'm sure they'd be honored to have you."

"Hmmm." I know that tone. I stifle a laugh.

There is a pause.

"Do you know where Medusa and Helen are?"

She lifts her eyes, somber with grief. "Of course, I do. And no, I am not going to tell you."

With that, she rises and leaves.

THIRTY

ODYSSEUS TAKES CONTROL

Callidice speaks

Of course, I cannot prevent him from finding my sisters. He is too wily for that.

One day as I sit with Pandora, helping the littlest sisters with their lessons, I hear screams and shouts coming from the arena, that sandy corner of the garden where all the executions have been carried out. We rise and run, finding ourselves in the shade of the tall trees that separate the garden from the arena.

Odysseus is there, dressed as the high-born lord he actually is, armed to the teeth, and sitting on Father's throne. Beside him sits

Medusa, a smile of glee warming her usually cold features. Before him stands Helen, surrounded by a horde of soldiers whom I do not recognize.

"They bear the Sigil of Ithaca," murmurs Pandora.

"But why are they here?"

"Because Lord Odysseus cannot trust Father's men."

I stare at her. Of course. Even if Father has now departed this earthly coil, that doesn't mean his men will trust Odysseus. Aloud I say, "This is a takeover. Odysseus has brought an army here, all the way from Ithaca."

"Medusa will be his bride. Surely *she* will help." Pandora does not smile.

My stomach knots into a fist. How dare she steal my suitor! How dare she take what is rightfully mine! *Except you don't want him,* the voice in my head reminds me.

Is that true? Do I really *not* want Odysseus?

You don't want to be married to a married man, the voice in my head remarks.

But Ithaca is so far away. Even if his wife is still living—

You would not mind? the voice in my head asks.

I close my eyes. Odysseus has not been in a hurry to return to Ithaca. Instead, he has spent the past year here, enduring our hospitality, or rather the lack of it. Why has he stayed?

You know the answer to that, the voice in my head avers.

My cheeks heat. If that is true, what is he doing with Medusa?

A sudden shout makes me turn. The men from Ithaca are proclaiming Odysseus as their King. "Oh-dih-seeh-US, oh-dih-seeh-US, oh-dih-seeh-US" they shout.

He rises to his feet as his men drag Helen before him. Even though her hands and feet are tightly bound, she favors him with a seductive smile, her allure radiating like tentacles slithering towards every man present. She is still the most beautiful woman in the world, with her glimmering dress, her shining hair a river of gold down her back.

Odysseus beckons and her maid appears to tame her hair into a thick plait. But she is sobbing so hard she cannot complete the task.

"Oh, let me!" Medusa hurls herself towards her sister, yanking her hair, and none-too-gently winding its brightness into a tight rope, which she pins up with long, lethal-looking pins.

Helen yelps and attempts to claw Medusa's face with her long, perfectly manicured nails. But the guards hold tight.

Finally, Medusa resumes her seat next to Odysseus. "There, my lord," she remarks. "She is yours to do with as you will."

His men force her to kneel. Someone puts a blindfold over her eyes, then the Ithacan soldiers step away, holding Helen still with long ropes as if she were a disobedient puppy on a leash.

Odysseus strides down from the dais, draws his sword, and begins whirling it around his head. When it is fast enough, he slices through Helen's slender neck.

Her head plops onto the floor with a sticky thunk, gushing rivers of blood.

Pandora and I scream, as we step behind the trees, our hands coming out to cover the eyes of out littlest sisters.

"YES!" Medusa leaps to her feet. Yes! Now that bitch is dead, I am First Lady—"

Odysseus's blade shoots out and stabs her through the heart. As she crumples to the blood-soaked sand, the snakes vanish. Seizing her hair, Odysseus separates her head from her body. Standing like a wall, he holds the heads of Helen and Medusa up in each hand, as his soldiers roar their approval.

I bend over, vomiting into the bushes. Then Pandora and I begin to usher the children back to the palace.

"Thus, do I avenge my son!" proclaims Odysseus, King of Ithaca, raising his dripping sword into the air.

His soldiers cheer.

"I am now the suitor who will rule Sikelia," he shouts. "I pledge myself to be the husband of Lady Callidice."

I freeze. Pandora puts her hand on my arm.

"We will marry tonight and rule this land together in peace and harmony."

The crowd parts as he comes to me, his clothing bespattered with my sisters' blood. Kneeling, he encircles my heart finger with a massive ruby ring.

Horrified, I am rooted to the spot as his soldiers put my sisters' heads on pikes, each adorning each side of the main gate, facing onto the street, where a crowd gathers in fascinated horror.

I retch again and again.

But Odysseus takes my hand. "Did you expect me *not* to avenge my son?"

"Noooo," I hear myself saying. I hate him for what he's done. But two destructive forces have been eliminated.

"I had to do this for you," he murmurs, kissing my hand. "To ensure your safety and that of our children."

I look up and melt. His eyes are so kind.

THIRTY-ONE

THE DREAM

Callidice speaks

Back in my chamber, I am torn apart by doubts. Could I really marry the man who had just murdered two of my sisters? How I would love to pace the room as that always spurs my thoughts. But my littlest sisters are fast asleep, exhausted from the trauma of the day. And so, I hunch up on my bed, hiding in the shadows.

Suppose I had been murdered instead? What would my sisters have done? It is easy to picture Medusa's possible actions. She would have gloried in my death, enjoyed watching it, and been smugly self-satisfied that I was out of the way and could no longer be a rival to her schemes.

But what about Helen? That is much harder to determine. As I let memories swirl over me, I realize that I do not know this sister well. She was so obvious in her sexuality, and in her desire to attract men. But what was really going on behind that lovely face? How I wish I knew.

I sigh as I draw my knees up to my chin. Could I have done anything to save Helen? I knew something terrible was going to happen, and yet I had been rooted to the spot, watching spellbound as those murderous events unfolded.

I retch again, but my stomach is empty. I haven't eaten anything today. I rise to my feet. What I really need is sleep, and so I mix up a sleeping potion, and crawl under the covers. Maybe Odysseus will go away, and I won't have to marry him after all.

While I slumber, my third sister Persephone, visits me in a dream. "You must marry," she says, taking my hands.

"But I cannot. You know what he did."

"You are the only one who can make matters right."

"But what about Pandora? She is the eldest."

She sighs, smiles and shakes her head. "Pandora is beyond marriage. She will never marry now. She will find her own way in the world."

"Doing what?"

"Being a powerful healer, of course."

"But her spells are no good—"

"I hear the Goddess Athena takes a great interest in our eldest sister. With her support, anything is possible."

"You mean," I say slowly, "she will leave, go to Athena's temple at Saragusa—"

"—join a community of women, become their leader and send powerful healers into this world," finishes Persephone.

"But men won't like that," I object

"She and her followers will be under the protection of Athena," replies Persephone.

"Men will not be able to do anything about it, at least not for several hundred years. Our sister will be safe and respected for her talents. She will be happy." Persephone stops and stares at me. "You wish for our sister to be happy?"

"Of course," I say. "But that doesn't mean I want to marry a murderer."

"You don't think he was justified?"

"Of course, he was justified!" I shout. "But it was truly horrifying what he did. He didn't have to do it in public, in front of them." I gulp down a sob. "In front of our littlest sisters." I bury my face in my hands and weep. I weep for myself, for what might have been if I had not had a crazy father. I weep for my sisters, especially for those who are no longer with us: Death-Bringer *Persephone,* Maiden *Kore,* and dearest Shadow *Briseis*. I even weep for Intrigue *Clytemnestra,* Shining *Helen,* and Protectress *Medusa*. At least All-Gifted *Pandora* will be happy. But what about the rest of us?

"Tonight," says Persephone once I quieten down, "you will take our sisters down through the grove of trees to the lake. You will invite your admirer King Odysseus to accompany you. Once there, you must do exactly as he says."

"What?" I sit up in my bed, the threads of the dream unraveling around me. "Why? How?"

But there is no answer. My sister has disappeared back into the Underworld.

THIRTY-TWO

THE RITE OF THE DEAD

Callidice speaks

As soon as I awaken, I send a message to Odysseus, requesting that he postpone our marriage by a day as I need his company this evening for an important visit.

He arrives within the hour, dressed as a prince, scowling as he enters our chamber. "What is this about postponing our marriage?" His voice is thick with fury.

I stop brushing Chryseis' hair and regard him. How very arrogant and presumptuous he is. But as I gaze at those steely grey eyes, my heart melts. He is angry because he thinks I have rejected him. And I am the only person in this room who has the power to appease him. Suddenly, all my doubts vanish. Yes, he has done terrible things, but everything he does has a reason. He is not mad like Father. Indeed, he is the sanest person I know. I take a deep breath. *I can handle this man,* I tell myself. And so, I rise to greet him, extending my hand for him to kiss.

"Persephone came to me in a dream just now."

His eyes narrow as he takes in our white robes, silver circlets threaded into our hair, and the jewels that wink from our throats, wrists and fingers.

"She wants you to accompany us to the castle."

"You want me to dance with you all night? That is not the sort of thing I care for."

I put my hand on his chest. "This is very important to all of us. And to me in particular."

He frowns down at me. "But I intend to marry you. Now."

I rise up onto my tiptoes, and kiss him on the lips, feeling a power thrum through me. "First, you are going to help me solve a puzzle." I have no idea where these words come from, but it is exactly the right thing to say.

His eyes soften, as he returns my kiss, long, full and passionate. "Lead on, my lady. I see I am to follow you to the ends of the earth."

I flick my fingers, and the spiral appears in the middle of the floor. I nod to Pandora, and she leads our sisters down, down, into its depths. First, Bow *Artemis,* followed by Sea-Foam *Aphrodite,* Ambiguity *Hecate,* and Treasure *Chryseis*. Odysseus bows and offers me his arm, and we come last.

As before, the torches flare to life as the floor-door grinds shut behind us. We follow the tunnel until we feel a thread of fresh air. Within moments, we are outside as the sun disappears behind the trees. Beside our feet a runnel springs to life, moving inexorably downwards as it grows into a stream, then a river, before ending with a roar into a plunging waterfall. We veer off to the side, walking downhill through the grove of magical trees until we come to the mirror-lake.

As before there are twelve boats, but the princes are unmasked. Pandora moves to the first boat and is greeted by a tall woman, with a high crown, and a breast-plate over her robes, holding a large shield in her left hand that is alive with snakes.

"That is the Goddess Athena," remarks Odysseus in my ear.

The second boat contains Medusa, but her snakes are gone and in their place her hair is done in an elaborate nest of plaits, which resemble snakes. Next to her sits an imposing man with a large, spade-shaped beard, bearing a trident in one hand. He glares at Athena.

"Lord Poseidon, God of the Sea," remarks Odysseus.

The third boat contains Persephone, her husband Lord Hades, God of the Underworld, and their daughter Princess Melinoë.

The fourth boat contains Helen and someone I do not know. "Menelaus, King of Sparta," says Odysseus.

"But—" I say. "I thought—." I don't dare to mention the part she played in Kousaleos' death."

"Helen is married to Menelaus," replies Odysseus. "I was one of her suitors, and it was my idea that all of her many suitors should swear a solemn oath that if anything befell her husband, the rest of us would come to his aid."

I stare at him. "I had no idea you were interested in Helen."

"I wasn't," he replies. "I wanted to marry her cousin Penelope."

"Of course," I murmur. *The long-suffering wife,* the voice in my head remarks.

Before I can ask more questions, Odysseus says, "Can you see your sister Kore in the fifth boat? The figure seated opposite is Hygieia, Goddess of Wellness and Hygiene."

I gaze at the goddess, taking in the snake coiled over her legs, contentedly sipping something from a bowl that Hygieia holds.

The sixth boat contains dearest Briseis, with a dark figure sitting opposite her.

"That is Erebus, Lord of Darkness," says Odysseus.

I shiver. "Is she happy?" I ask. "What is her life like?"

"Her husband protects her," replies Odysseus kissing my fingers one by one. "She is safe."

I want to ask more, but we arrive at the seventh boat. Odysseus bows and hands me in, taking up the oars and rowing with expert strokes across the lake.

He catches me looking at him. "I am a sailor at heart," he smiles. "Ithaca is an island, and so my people are great sea-farers."

The eighth boat contains Clytemnestra and another figure I do not recognize. "Agamemnon, King of Mycenae," says Odysseus.

I frown. "But I thought—." Suddenly, I cannot bear to tell him that Clytemnestra was going to marry Father. My cheeks heat so much even my ears become warm.

Odysseus smiles grimly. "Clytemnestra is very much like her sister Helen. Just as Helen has been married to Menelaus from an early age, so Clytemnestra has been married to Agamemnon. He is the greatest war-lord alive. He was the leader of the Greeks during the Trojan War."

Something slides into place. Something that one of my sisters said during my last visit. "Helen started the Trojan War."

Odysseus sighs. "Indeed, she did. She was the loveliest woman in the world, and many vied for her hand in marriage."

"But it was your idea that all of her suitors should help her husband."

He raises a brow. "I had to come up with something to prevent them from fighting like stray dogs over her."

"But a war erupted nevertheless," I say.

But I do not get a chance to continue, for he touches my arm. "Look at your little sister Artemis, with Apollo, Lord Oracle. He speaks through the Pythia, the snake-woman at Delphi."

Goodness, I say to myself. *Everywhere I turn I see snakes. The Greeks are obsessed with them*. But my attention is diverted by the exalted company my littlest sisters keep. Not only has Artemis acquired Apollo, but Aphrodite sits with Ares, Lord War in the tenth boat, while the eleventh boat contains Hecate and Osiris, Lord Afterlife. Lastly, in the twelfth boat, our baby sister Chryseis has gained the greatest prize of all, for her companion is Zeus, Lord Deity.

One by one, our boats travel across the lake towards the gleaming castle. As before, our princes hand us out of each boat and we climb the castle steps that lead into the ballroom. But before the magical threads of flute and drum can swirl around us, a voice calls "Halt!"

Lord Charon appears, bowing low. "Welcome again to the Bardo, the land of the in-between. I send especial greetings tonight to Princess Callidice and Lord Odysseus with my best wishes for your forthcoming nuptials." He bows low to Odysseus, who smiles in return.

"When last you were here," continues Charon, "you had the honor of meeting Gilgamesh, one of our great kings of old. I am sure you will be glad to know that he survived his travails and is with us today." Again, he bows low before Odysseus.

"Here is Gilgamesh," proclaims Charon, opening his arm to indicate Odysseus.

"You are Gilgamesh?" I exclaim. "You look nothing like him."

"Someone is writing a poem about my travels," replies Odysseus. "And someone else is writing a poem about Gilgamesh called *The Epic of Gilgamesh*. The two are quite similar."

I stare at him. "What is your poem called?"

"*The Odyssey,*" he replies.

This poem must be about what happened to him after the Trojan War ended. It must be about the many people - women - I correct myself he must have met. Is this why it has taken him fourteen years to come home? Did he leave a young family behind to return to Ithaca? *This will be your future,* the voice in my head remarks. But suddenly, I don't want to know.

"You have become a hero," I remark.

He kneels before me. "I am *your* hero." He kisses each finger as he gazes into my eyes.

We are interrupted by a cough, and Lord Charon comes forward holding a silver goblet in his hand, which he offers to Odysseus, who drinks deeply.

He proffers the cup to me, but I shake my head. "I don't want drugged wine," I say. "Look at what happened to my sisters' suitors. They were executed after drinking it."

"Lord Charon is healing us with Lethe, with the waters of forgetfulness, so that when we return to the land of the living, we can start anew."

I look up into his grey eyes, now as frank as a mountain stream. "I trust you," I say slowly, realizing with surprise that what I say is true. And so, I take the cup he holds out to me, and drink deep also. Each of my sisters drinks, and the cup is returned to Charon.

"My lords and ladies, let us form a circle and perform the rite of the dead."

As we begin, the castle disintegrates, melting before our eyes. We are in a temple, surrounded by a large cave.

"This is the sanctuary of Demeter," says Charon, "the goddess mother of Persephone. The life-giving goddess of grains and cereals. We must pour our libations here and dance our holy prayers."

Again, the silver cup is passed around for us to sprinkle a few drops of wine before our feet, chanting the names of the dead as we do so. Then the haunting sound of the reed flute and the driving rhythm of the drum entice us into dance. Holding hands, we dance from left to right and then from right to left and sing:

Dawn veiled in saffron, arise from the waves of the ocean,

Carry light to the immortals and to mortal men

One by one, in order of death, my sisters place themselves in the middle of our circle. First, Persephone, her daughter in her arms, her husband by her side turns this way and that as a writhing wind plucks at her hair and robes. As the wind subsides, they slowly vanish like water dripping from a water clock.

She is followed by Intrigue, dearest Briseis, Kore, Helen, and Medusa.

When all of our dead sisters are gone, Odysseus leads us through a maze of tunnels until we come up and out to see a familiar sight. Our castle, with our tower pointing up like a finger, standing proud as it surveys the surrounding countryside.

"The curse has ended," says Odysseus, as we breathe in the fresh air of the early hours before dawn. "The goddess was furious with your father for building his castle over her temple. So, she punished him by making his daughters dance all night long."

"But why did she make us dance?"

"You were dancing your prayers to her, pleading with her to let you go. But she refused. Until I arrived."

"Because you are the hero," I say, smiling up at him.

We kiss.

THIRTY-THREE

EPILOGUE

Callidice speaks

Our nuptials took place a few hours later, just as the sky turned rose-gold and the disk of the sun arced high into the sky.

Odysseus and I pledged to love one another, to treat each other with respect, and to care for one another through illness until death.

Then we went out into the garden to greet the people, who mirrored our joy with their cheers.

My Odysseus made one more promise to me on our wedding night. He promised to stay as long as needful, until all of my remaining sisters had found husbands, or were otherwise settled. As Treasure, my youngest sister, had just turned six, I comforted myself with the knowledge that he would remain by my side for many a long year.

But all-too-soon the day came when he bid me farewell. By that time our eldest child had seven years, and so I acted as Regent until she reached her majority at the age of twenty-one years. She married a pleasant young man who was the weaker partner in their relationship, for I saw to it that my eldest, my Polyxena, would not have her rule challenged by anyone, least of all her husband.

By then, I possessed forty autumns, and that winter caught a chill and died. I died with a smile on my lips knowing that my task was done, my children were safe, and that the youngest ones had good people to guide them. I died knowing I would meet my loved ones again: Shadow, All-Gifted, Death-Bringer, and Maiden.

Of Odysseus, I had no knowledge.

May he find peace also.

Would You Like to be an Advanced Reader?

You'll receive a FREE book and other bonuses!
MEMBERSHIP includes:

a free book
advance review copies
newsletter.

Subscribe here ~
https://cynthiasallyhaggard.com/contact/
(and tap WIP Updates)

Your opinion is important to me...

Thank you for reading *Maiden Tomb*.

Reviews are so important because they allow people like me (an unknown Indie author) to find people like you (readers who enjoy historical fiction.)

An unreviewed book is like a rose gasping for water.

So if you enjoyed *Maiden Tomb*, you would make one author very happy by posting a short review at your favorite online retailer.

It only takes 5 minutes...

Thank you so much for your support!

Warmly, Cynthia

As a Thank You ~

for reading *Maiden Tomb,*
(the first in a series of books in my
forthcoming *Twelve Cursed Maidens* series)
I am going to share an excerpt
from the beginning of *Maiden Forgotten,*
the second in the series

Book Two in the Twelve Cursed Maidens series

MAIDEN FORGOTTEN

Would you promote your daughters if you were the Greatest King in the Whole World, but your sons promised to be utterly unworthy successors?

CYNTHIA SALLY HAGGARD

PROLOGUE~ SHADOWS

The Monastery of Longquan
Phoenix Mountains
Northern China
18 December 1271

Shadow speaks

I am old, I am wizened, I am gnarled and unattractive. But I have stories to tell. I have met men who possess the flames of ambition in their eyes. Even more unusual, I have met remarkable women, women who lives soared beyond the commonplace, women who exceeded what was thought possible for them, at least in the eyes of their men. For when I was still very young,

I met two queens who ruled their fortress kingdoms along the Silk Road.

They were the daughters of Chinggis Khan, the most terrifying conqueror the world has ever seen. That man—that monster—was unusually cruel to those who crossed him. But he loved his daughters, making splendid matches for them. The third daughter, whose name has come down to us as Alakhai Bekhi (her family called her Ambiguity), married the Ongud lord. Normally, she would have sat subserviently by her husband's side, a queen consort and no more. But her father sent her husbands away on dangerous missions, ensuring that from the very day she arrived in Ongud territory, she ruled as queen. Her younger sister, Al-Altan (or Treasure), married the Uighur lord. Again, her father ensured that her new husband was busy fighting for him while she queened it in Beshbalik, at the foothills of the Tianshan Mountains, close to the northern arm of the Silk Road.

During my long, long life, I have borne many names. None of them matter anymore, as the people who called me by those names are long dead. But you should know, dear reader, that for most of my adult life, I went by the name of Shadow. For that is the nickname bestowed upon me by that great conqueror Chinggis Khan. (He was grateful for the small part I played in saving the life of Queen Ambiguity.)

It was Queen Ambiguity herself who turned my nickname to advantage, for she noticed that I was adept at fading into invisibility, into the shadows cast by lanterns, candles, or the gathering storm outside.

And so, while self-important men strutted like peacocks in front of my queen, I would curl up out of sight upon a cushion, embroidering a pillow or some such item, silently clawing back each word that was spoken, so that I might repeat it back to Queen Ambiguity afterwards. When a pause ensued, I would look up and judge his body language. Why was he silent? Was he unsure? Embarrassed? Or was he hiding something? All of these things would be stowed away in the recesses of my mind to be brought forth later on, during those long, too-quiet evenings, when my mistress wished for my advice.

In later years, I made the long journey from the court of Queen Ambiguity in northern China to the Province of Xinjiang to serve her younger sister, Queen Treasure.

I close my eyes and do a breath meditation to quieten my mind before picking up my brush and dipping it back into my ink pot. For what I have to say now is achingly painful.

One of these sisters was the love of my life. The other I served more out of a sense of duty. Even so, I tried to remain loyal to each of them until the end. I was at the deathbed of one, the execution of the other. Even now, I suffer sleepless nights wondering if I could have done more to prevent the murder of Chinggis Khan's favorite daughter.

I draw in a deep breath to quell the memories that have given me nightmares these many years. The kindly men and women who inhabit this Buddhist monastery in the mountains (near a large city whose names are various) tell me that I have been punished enough. That my queens never blamed me for the disasters that befell them. That they knew I would have laid down my life, many times, in their stead. That now that I am in the winter of my life, I must let such dark thoughts go.

And so, I pick up my brush anew, dip it in ink, and form new characters on the clean area of scrolled paper to my left. For before death comes to claim me, I must write everything down about these sisters and their extraordinary lives.

About Cynthia

Cynthia Sally Haggard was born and reared in Surrey, England. About 40 years ago, she surfaced in the United States, inhabiting the Mid-Atlantic region as she wound her way through four careers: violinist, cognitive scientist, medical writer, and novelist.

Her first novel, *Thwarted Queen*, a saga about the Yorks, Lancasters & Nevilles, whose family feud inspired "Game of Thrones," won the 2021 Gold Medal IPPY Award for Audiobook, with the fab Diana Croft narrating. Her second novel, *Farewell My Life,* a dark historical about a hidden murderer, won the 2021 Independent Press Award for Women's Fiction and was the 2019 Distinguished Favorite for the New York City Big Book Award.

Cynthia graduated with an MFA in Creative Writing from Lesley University, Cambridge MA, in June 2015.

When she's not annoying everyone by insisting her fictional characters are more real than they are, Cynthia likes to go for long walks, knit something glamorous, cook in her wonderful kitchen, and play the piano.

You can visit her at cynthiasallyhaggard.com

Websites

Facebook

https://www.facebook.com/cynthiasallyhaggardnovelist/

Instagram

https://www.instagram.com/cynthia_at_cynthia_sally/

Pinterest

https://www.pinterest.com/cynthiasallyhaggard/

LinkedIn

https://www.linkedin.com/in/cynthiasallyhaggard/

Website

https://www.cynthiasallyhaggard.com/about/

www.ingramcontent.com/pod-product-compliance
Lightning Source LLC
LaVergne TN
LVHW090555110826
845146LV00001B/137

* 9 7 9 8 9 8 5 4 9 6 9 6 3 *